Catherine

I0618147

By Sue Barr

Published by: Susan L Barr

D2D Print ISBN: 978-1-393-93370-0

Cover Design: the Midnight Muse

Some secrets are not meant to be shared.

Catherine Bennet knows this better than anyone and the one she carries will remain hidden forever. This means she'll never marry and it never bothered her before she met Lord George. He's determined to breach the walls of defense so carefully constructed around her heart and she's just as determined to stay the course.

Some secrets cannot be shared

An agent for the Crown, Lord George Kerr, concealed his espionage activities beneath a blanket of gossip, drink and loose women. Though forced to resume a more mundane lifestyle among London's finest, he covertly seeks a traitor to England. All trails seem to converge around Miss Catherine Bennet, a reticent country miss, who unwittingly has captured his heart.

Some things are beyond your control

With the very lives of England's vast network of spies working undercover in Bonaparte's France hanging in the balance, Catherine is forced to face her worst nightmare. Her secret laid bare, can George love her enough to overcome what he learns?

SUE BARR

To Jane Austen
Without her wonderful book, Pride & Prejudice.
this work of fiction would never have been created

CATHERINE

To Rob
*You are **my** Mr. Darcy*
I love you more than black jellybeans

Chapter One

London

L The drawing room was quiet, save for the shuffling of papers and every now and then a soft, yet impatient sigh.

"Darling, as much as I love my own company, I am feeling a trifle neglected."

Lord George Kerr shifted his attention from the documents spread out before him toward the beautiful woman seated across the room. He appreciated the way the crimson brocade couch acted as a perfect foil for her exotic features and raven hair.

"Evangeline, you know our agreement. I attend your exquisite establishment and you whisk me away to your sumptuous parlor, whereupon I gather information for King and Country." He grinned at her sultry pout. "Now be a pet and make some noise. Otherwise your servants will gossip I am not here for a lover's tryst and that would be disastrous for our partnership."

"If you only knew how envious my maids are. Miss Bledsoe told me they remain convinced you are Casanova reincarnated. Imagine their surprise if they knew we only drink tea and talk." She arose from the couch and glided behind his chair, combing long fingers through his hair. "Could I not entice you, just this once?"

He stilled her hand and brought her palm to his lips. Pressing a kiss against the soft skin, he murmured, "While I admire your tenacity, I cannot give what you ask. The only woman I will share a bed with will be my future wife."

"I did not say we had to be in a bed."

"Evangeline," he warned in a low voice.

"Very well, for you I shall behave." She turned aside with an elegant shrug of her slim shoulders and moved toward the picture hung over the fireplace. For a brief moment she stared at the portrait of her husband. "I miss that man more than words can say." She tensed and looked toward the door. "Someone is coming."

She moved swiftly to the couch. Without questioning her instinct, which had proven itself time and again, he laid his coat on top of the papers and joined her, positioning his body so that his head rested on her lap. He placed his left foot on the cushioned seat, knee slightly bent, and stretched the right leg to the floor. She glanced down at him, her delicate features tight with concern.

"Prepare yourself, Lord George. In order to facilitate our ruse as lovers, I must expose more than you would like."

"I believe I shall somehow survive," he replied in a dry tone.

She slipped the filmy gown down one arm and it puddled gracefully against his cheek. The door to the salon burst open and her lady's companion, Miss Bledsoe, the only one who knew of their true connection, trembled within the door frame. Behind her stood two men with hardened faces and what George presumed were loaded pistols. A quick glance past the two men revealed Evangeline's aged butler crumpled on the floor in the front vestibule.

"What is the meaning of this?" Evangeline demanded. She tugged the gown back onto her shoulder while George remained where he lay, a deceptive picture of languor and satisfied coitus.

"I'm sorry, Lady Anstruther..." Miss Bledsoe began.

"Quiet, slut." The larger man growled and backhanded her.

With a cry, Miss Bledsoe stumbled against the smaller man, who grabbed her wrist in a vice-like grip. When he saw her face, his eyes lit up.

"Look who we have here," he crowed, a vicious grin twisting his mouth.

Miss Bledsoe ducked her head and tried to pull away, only to cry out again when the man tightened his grip. If Evangeline noticed Smithson laying on the vestibule floor, she gave no indication.

"Not this time. You made him very angry by running away and he'll pay a nice tidy sum for your return."

Although piqued by the smaller man's comment, George focused on the fact his voice and manners were too cultured and a hint of familiarity tugged at the recesses of his mind. Evangeline pushed his head off her lap and arose in an apparent state of agitation. George, still semi-reclined, slid the hand hidden from sight down toward his boot.

"Please do not harm my companion," she begged and stumbled, steadying herself by gripping the back of the divan. "Why are you here?"

He was familiar with this ruse because she'd done it to him in France. She intended to retrieve the weapon strapped to the back of the divan. Distracted by her nervous display, neither man observed him unsheathe a knife and palm the deadly weapon.

"If they so much as twitch, kill them." The smaller man called over his shoulder, tugging Miss Bledsoe behind him. "Shoot the prancing dandy first."

"With pleasure Reggie," the larger man growled and bared his yellow teeth in a sickening grin.

Reggie continued toward the table and it was only through years of conditioning that George didn't betray concern he would discover smuggled documents. If these men escaped with the knowledge of his and Evangeline's clandestine operation, then many courageous people would have died for nothing. It was time for him to act.

He arose from the couch like a sleepy giant.

"You hafta wait your turn," he slurred out, weaving on his feet as though drunk. "I pay a lot of money for her exclusive favors. You can have her when I'm done."

"You dare to pass me off to these... these ruffians?" Evangeline raged and stomped her foot, the pistol hidden against her side.

Her tantrum had the desired effect. The larger man momentarily shifted his attention from George to Evangeline. Without hesitation, George whipped the blade toward him. Surprised, the thug stared at his chest. At first there was nothing to see except the hilt of the dagger, then like the incoming tide, a dark red stain began to spread across his dingy shirt. In a matter of seconds, he sank to his knees, dropped the gun and crumpled to the ground.

At the sound of his accomplice hitting the floor, Reggie turned and pulled Miss Bledsoe tight against his side, but before he could even point his weapon, Evangeline had raised her arm. With deadly aim she made sure he never breathed again. When Reggie fell to the floor, Miss Bledsoe ran to her friend's side.

George assessed the bullet hole dead square in Reggie's forehead, marveling at Evangeline's accuracy. As good as he was with any weapon of any kind, even he wouldn't attempt a shot like that with someone standing so close.

"Remind me to never challenge you to a duel, Countess."

Evangeline lowered her arm and cut him a sideways glance. "You are most fortunate I adore you, otherwise that may have been you on the floor after offering to share my favors."

"It was a means to an end." He took hold of her free hand and brought it to his lips, murmuring against her skin. "I am forever grateful you did not shoot me in France."

"Bah, Cavendish was right, you are a terrible flirt." She tugged her hand from his light grasp and hurried to the vestibule. By the time she'd reached his side, Smithson had begun to groan and move about. "Miss Bledsoe. Please have a footman fetch my physician." Once she and George had settled Smithson in another room, she turned to him. "Come, let us find out who those two Cretans were."

"I AM AFRAID YOUR COVER has been compromised." Lord Patrick Grayson, Marquis of Chadwick, clasped his hands on his desk and peered at George over his reading glasses. "You are quite useless to us now."

"I should like to know who sent those men."

George sat in the chair placed directly in front of Lord Grayson's desk. His one elbow rested on the arm of the chair and he rhythmically rubbed his lower lip with his index finger. A childhood habit indicating deep thought.

He and Evangeline had searched both men thoroughly, finding no form of identification or written instructions on either of them. The larger man definitely had been a thug for hire, but the cultured tones and soft hands of 'Reggie' hinted at a decent education and no hard labor. Had he been the leader or following someone else's orders? The same sense of familiarity washed over George.

His attempts to speak with Miss Bledsoe resulted in her bursting into tears. Evangeline indicated she would speak with her when they were alone, and with great reluctance, he'd backed off.

"I would like to know who they were as well." Lord Grayson removed his glasses and pinched the bridge of his nose. "At times, I think there are more people working for Boney in England than in France. Money and a skewered devotion to ancient family ties can turn even the most patriotic away from their King. Look at what has happened in our very own country. The Prime Minister, assassinated."

"Nasty business, that. I am still not convinced there was no conspiracy." George rose to his feet and paced to the large Palladian window, clasping his hands behind his back. "So, what am I to do? Become another useless younger brother to a Peer of the realm?"

"You do yourself a disservice, Lord George. Your family name has a proud history and the *ton* have no idea you worked for the Crown. For all they care you are still their golden boy who sowed more than his share of wild oats. Continue on with your life. Find a pretty girl and get married. It would make the Duke a happy man if you settled down."

"Maxwell would be ecstatic if I entered into marital bliss." George turned to face Lord Grayson. "Unfortunately, I have played the part of a Rake so convincingly, all good mothers hide their daughters as soon as I enter a ballroom."

"As the brother of a Duke, you and I both know your reputation will not stop them from wanting an association with your family."

"All they see is my connections and fortune. I desire to meet someone fresh and new. Someone who is not skilled with the arts and allurements used to ensnare a husband."

"Look at this as a blessing. Now that you no longer have to look over your shoulder and peer into every dark corner for the enemy, you can enjoy the full social whirl. With your charm and exceedingly handsome visage, you will have no problem securing a nice young lady."

George doubted that very much but didn't have the heart to contradict his friend and mentor. All this talk of meeting eligible wives gave him a roaring headache. He'd take a rough and tumble spy any day to a cunning mother on the hunt for a son-in-law.

"What of my contact here in London? Do you have anyone who can continue on with our work?" He deftly moved the conversation away from the delicate subject of marriage onto something more pressing, and in his mind, not as dangerous.

"Sadly, no. Not many men, or women are willing to live a secret life. As you are the only person who knew their identity,

I shall leave you to inform them of our decision to retire you." Lord Grayson rose from his chair and extended a hand toward George, who returned from the window and shook it firmly. "It was a pleasure to work with you, Lord George. I wish you a long and healthy life."

"Thank you, Lord Grayson. Might I add, it was an honor to serve my country and if you ever require my services, you need only send word and I will be there."

"I know you would, lad. I know you would. Since Percival's assassination, we live in perilous times and we need all those who are loyal to the Monarchy."

Within minutes, George exited the offices where Lord Grayson conducted his business and approached a nondescript carriage manned by his trusted driver, Henry.

"Where to, m'lord?"

"Kerr house."

"Yes, sir."

George entered the carriage, settling onto the comfortable bench. Henry closed the carriage door and climbed up to his seat at the front. He flicked the reins and the horses took off at a brisk pace toward Mayfair. George used the time to reflect on the past few days. He'd hired some private investigators, ones he trusted and had used before, to scour the area for any leads. With a touch of luck, he hoped they'd ascertain the identity of Reggie and who his connections were.

He'd instructed the men to be discreet with their inquiries as spies had a tendency to hide. He should know – he'd been hiding in plain sight for almost five years.

CATHERINE

"MY LORD, I HAD NOT expected to see you again."

Evangeline greeted George with a kiss on the cheek before inviting him to follow her to the main parlor. He handed his hat, gloves and top coat to Evangeline's new butler, MacDougal, a burly Scot who never broke a smile. He'd moved up from under-butler when Smithson became injured. One would have to be a fool if they didn't realize he was more of a bodyguard than a butler.

Without a sound she opened the door to the front parlor and made for the tray where clean glasses and expensive, smuggled brandy waited. Other than a new rug in the middle of the room, there was no visible sign that two men had died a violent death here. She didn't ask if he wanted a drink, she just poured some amber liquid into two tumblers and handed him one.

"Have you found out who the thief was?" She moved toward the couch and sat down while George took the chair opposite.

"Not a single clue, although I began some discreet inquiries through secure channels. I hate waiting about but Mother is pleased with my enforced company. Since my wings have been clipped, so to speak, she has encouraged me to escort her to a few teas and afternoon soirees. I shudder to think of what she has in store when the Season gets into full swing. 'Tis only a matter of time before she begins to pester me about taking over Keswick Manor and managing the property."

"I am sure she will pester you about more than managing your future estate. Your mother is hungry for grandchildren and wishes to bounce a few babies on her knee while still young enough to enjoy them. Poor George, such a hard life you lead." She chuckled at his grimace and sipped her drink, closing her

eyes as the alcohol made its way down her throat. "Mmmm....
As much as I abhor the French, they do have excellent port
brandy."

"Has Miss Bledsoe recovered from the incident?"

"Although extremely nervous for a few days, she has since
settled. One does not like the sound of a bullet whizzing by
their ear. It reminds us of our own mortality."

"None of us live forever." He assessed his friend, perched so
politely on the divan, the embodiment of alluring femininity.
"I still do not know how you did it. If I had not seen it with my
own eyes, no one would convince me you were that good of a
shot."

"There are many things you don't know about me Lord
George, and until that imposter is removed from France and
my Cavendish is returned to me, I dare not share my story."

"Has Miss Bledsoe mentioned anything which might help
us discover Reggie's identity?"

"That is a dead-end street. Women have many reasons for
entering into a life of servitude and sometimes their motive is
personal and fraught with danger. I will never divulge her secret. I am sure you understand."

Yes, he did. Keeping secrets was something he understood
only too well. He placed his untouched drink on the side table
and leaned forward until his forearms rested on his thighs.

"I do not know if our operation was compromised." He
held Evangeline's gaze. "And there are too many loose ends
here. It is not safe to continue."

"I thought as much." She didn't show surprise at his statement and he wondered what, exactly, Miss Bledsoe shared with
her.

"Let us begin to circulate among our friends that we were never lovers, only good friends. When Cavendish returns, it will be much easier on you if the *ton* believe you have been a virtuous wife, which is the truth."

"You mean you shall conceal my moment of weakness, where I almost begged you to take me to bed?" she teased.

"I knew you were not serious. You have only had eyes for Cavendish from the moment you met him."

"You are a good man, George. What will you do with yourself, without all this intrigue to spur your imagination?" Her eyes sparkled with mischief as she relaxed against the back of her chair, rolling the glass between her hands. After three years of working together, she was comfortable in his presence.

"I have a friend getting married in Derbyshire the first week of November and the Duke and I are invited to attend. Our brother Nathan resides in a small village near our friend's estate, so I shall force my company on him, enjoy the country air and maybe learn how to raise sheep." He rose to his feet, took possession of Evangeline's fingers and raised them to his lips. "I bid you adieu."

"Stay safe, dear friend," she murmured, withdrawing her hand from his.

"I shall endeavor to do my very best and wish you success with your re-entry into Society."

Chapter Two

Wedding Breakfast of Fitzwilliam Darcy and Elizabeth Bennet
and Charles Bingley and Jane Bennet

Catherine Bennet, better known as Kitty to family and close friends, could barely eat, so consumed was she by nervousness. The multitude of Lords and Ladies gathered around the table made her feel as if they were in St. James Court instead of the formal dining hall at Pemberley

Across from her sat Miss Georgiana Darcy, with whom she felt a real kinship, and to Miss Darcy's left was Maxwell Kerr, the Fifth Duke of Adborough. Further down the table sat the Earl and Countess of Matlock, the Marquis of Dorchester, and a host of other nobility. Although the room fairly burst with members of the beau monde from London's society, none of them filled her as much disquiet as the gentleman on her immediate right.

Lord George Kerr.

Never had she met someone who was so attractive. Not even Jane with all her serene beauty came close. Their Father in Heaven must have been feeling most generous when He formed this man. At that exact moment, to her utter dismay, Lord Kerr turned his attention from the Dowager Viscountess

Dalrymple on his right side toward her. Unprepared for his direct attention, she froze. Almost against her will, her gaze zeroed in on his mouth which had begun to move.

Oh, dear heaven. He said something, yet the blood rushing in and around her ears drowned out all sound. Then, that sensuous mouth curved into a slight smile revealing perfectly even, white teeth. She ducked her head and concentrated on her bowl of soup, hoping against hope her face hadn't flared a crimson red, for then he would think she was a gauche child and not a young lady of eight and ten. When her composure returned, she risked another glance and caught him watching.

Confound the man! Why must he still look her way? Was he not hungry? Did he have nothing better to do than discompose her so completely? With great care she dipped her spoon into the savory broth.

"Did you enjoy the wedding ceremony, Miss Catherine?"

Startled, she sloshed a bit of soup over the side of her spoon. Even his voice was heavenly, all deep and rumbly and flowed like rum sauce over one of Mama's Christmas puddings. Counting to five, because that's what Lizzy once told her to do when nervous, she willed her nerves to settle. All she had to do was maintain her composure and behave as though dining with near royalty was a common occurrence.

"I did. I am very happy for my sister and Mr. Darcy."

She turned her attention back to the soup and steadfastly ignored the rapid staccato of her heart. However, Lord Kerr continued to engage her in conversation, seemingly oblivious that she was nothing but a pile of nerves. A very hungry pile of nerves. In the mad rush to get Lizzy and Jane to the church on time, after a fit of vapors by Mama, she'd had nothing to eat all day.

"I have not had the pleasure of being properly introduced to your sister. She and Darcy seem well suited."

He reached for his glass of wine. Unlike her, he had no problem eating and conversing. This would not do. At this rate she'd die of starvation. She almost sighed in relief when the footman whisked away her untouched soup and placed in front of her the second course.

"Lizzy and Mr. Darcy are very well suited," she replied. "They both have strong opinions and are not afraid to voice them. Some of their future breakfasts will be very interesting."

Lord Kerr laughed out loud at her observation, causing more than one head to turn in their direction. She reached for a glass of water, grateful her trembling was not too visible and took a sip. Papa always said she was a silly girl and here she was, proving him right by embarrassing herself in front of important strangers.

Lord Kerr picked up a knife and fork and sliced into the meat on his plate. Surreptitiously, she cut a sideways glance to see which cutlery he used. Why did there have to be so many forks and spoons and knives lining the perimeter of her place setting? Mama always put up such lovely dinners, but none of them compared to the pomp and ceremony here at Pemberley.

Her stomach rumbled in protest. Lord Kerr turned slightly and smiled again.

"You are famished. Why are you not eating?"

Embarrassed, she stared at the thick slices of ham on her dinner plate and tears threatened to trickle down her cheeks. Out of the corner of her eye she noticed him tapping one of his forks and when her left hand touched the proper one he gave a slight nod.

"Thank you," she murmured.

"You are welcome," he whispered back.

Less than two hours later, standing near the French doors which led out to a pretty terrace, Kitty surveyed the rolling grounds of Pemberley. After the hustle and bustle of the morning where her nerves had been stretched to near breaking, she was glad for this respite, away from the busy parlors where most of the guests still lingered.

She blew out a small sigh.

Other than the plethora of elevated guests, the wedding had been perfect. When saying their vows, Lizzy and Jane had positively glowed, and one couldn't miss the soft looks of love that Mr. Darcy and Mr. Bingley bestowed on each of their brides.

As happy as she was for her eldest sisters, she couldn't wait for all the excitement to die down. Once Elizabeth and Mr. Darcy, and Jane and Mr. Bingley exited for their wedding trip, she and Mary planned to escape to their rooms and talk about the day. She rested her head against the window frame and with eyes closed, willed her soul to quiet.

"Miss Bennet, we did not get to finish our conversation in the dining room."

For the second time that day, she gave a small start. In the midst of her daydreaming, she hadn't heard anyone enter the room.

"Lord Kerr."

For such a large man he moved with stealth and grace. She turned and gave him a polite curtsy.

"You may call me Lord George, if you like. Otherwise Nathan and sometimes even Maxwell will answer you as he is not accustomed to being called 'Your Grace,'" he teased and stopped a few feet from where she stood.

"Oh… of course. Thank you, Lord George."

The silence stretched long between them and she twisted her fingers together, determined to *not* clutch her skirt and wrinkle the fine material. She cast about for something to say. Anything to break the awkward silence.

"Are you pleased—"

"How long are you—"

Both spoke at the same time.

"Pray, excuse me Miss Bennet. Please continue." He gave her a quick nod.

"I was going to ask you if you were pleased with your brother's announcement, after Lizzy and Darcy's banns were read the third and final time."

"You are speaking of his engagement to Miss Bingley?"

"Yes, it came as quite the surprise to most of us."

"I must admit I have never met the lady, but then I only arrived the evening previous and have not had much time to converse with my younger brother."

"In some ways your brother will become part of our extended family." At his quizzical expression, she explained further. "Miss Bingley's brother, Charles is now married to my sister Jane."

"Ah, the Angel of Hertfordshire he sighs about."

She stifled a giggle. "Mr. Bingley is quite besotted, as is she."

"How long are you and your family staying at Pemberley?"

"We leave this coming Thursday. With Lizzy and Mr. Darcy away on their wedding trip, Papa made the decision to return home, although I am sure he'd like to stay longer, if only to enjoy the library."

"Pemberley does have a massive library. Generations of Darcy's have contributed to the contents." He gave her another one of his beatific smiles. "And you. Will you miss anything from Pemberley?"

Kitty paused and thought for a few moments. "I shall miss the grounds. I do not walk as often as Lizzy, but I enjoy a ramble every now and then and the gardens are beautiful."

"That they are. I am staying with my brother Nathan for a few days—"

"Kitty!" Mrs. Bennet called from the doorway, unmindful that she was in conversation with Lord George. For the first time in her young life she became aware of her mother's coarse behavior and felt exposed in front of him. "Come quickly. Lizzy and Mr. Darcy are leaving."

"I must go, sir." Cheeks flaming, she performed a quick curtsy and turned to follow her mother, faltering only slightly in her progress when she thought she heard him say.

"I hope to see you again, Miss Catherine."

GEORGE STIFLED THE urge to pace the dining room of White's while waiting for his brother Max. Months of sitting around, doing nothing was slowly driving him to distraction. With the death of their Uncle Moreland and his wife last November, not long after Darcy's wedding, the family had entered into half mourning. This precipitated delaying Nathan's wedding to Miss Bingley and curtailed any Yuletide balls or afternoon soirees where the sharks circled. However, Mother still demanded he escort her or appear at some of her quiet afternoon teas with close friends. Close friends who happened to have marriageable daughters in attendance.

In a few short weeks a new crop of debutantes would make their curtsy before the Queen and the High Season would begin. To avoid his mother, whose unsubtle hints that he should marry and take over Keswick Manor increased daily, he'd begun to stay at his own lodgings.

That was, until this morning.

He'd received what amounted to a royal command to attend breakfast at Kerr House. Over a delicious spread of ham, sausages and eggs, Mother had demanded that he 'do' something with his life. Unwilling to disappoint, yet also unwilling to dance attendance to a group of insipid, entitled young ladies, he promised to meet with Max when he came to London and discuss property management.

His attention was diverted by his brother entering the dining room.

"It is good to see you, Max." George rose to his feet and extended a hand in greeting.

"Same here, brother. It has been ages since I have been away from Adborough Hall." Max waved his hand aside and gave him a brotherly hug instead.

"I am glad you arrived," George said as they broke apart. "I, for one, am hungry."

Several minutes later they were seated and served.

"Have you managed to settle Uncle Moreland's estate?" George asked as he cut into his roasted pheasant.

"Almost. My solicitors are searching for the rightful heir. The cousin who inherited is in the army and was sent to the Canada's last year. They are attempting to ferret out where the good lieutenant is and if he is still alive." Max signaled a footman.

"May I get you anything, Your Grace?" the footman asked with a respectful bow.

"Some more port wine."

"Right away."

"What was I saying?" Max turned his attention back to George.

"Your solicitors were trying to find Uncle Moreland's heir who is in the thick of battle in the colonies. What happens if he is deceased?"

"You will not believe this, but Nathan inherits."

"How?" George almost choked on his wine. He lowered the glass, wiped his mouth with a white linen napkin.

"As you know, Uncle Moreland's estate is not entailed and he bequeathed it to his brother's son and his heir, if there is one. The estate falls to Nathan if the line is broken."

"We are talking about our brother Nathan, the one who gave up everything to join the church?"

"One and the same." Max lifted a napkin to his mouth, but George could tell he was smiling as well.

"Oh, that is rich. If he does inherit, can I be there when you tell him?"

"No."

"Please."

"No."

"Since you became the Duke, you are no longer any fun."

"You, my brother, have more fun than all of us combined. I have heard tales of you skirting the edges of good moral standing. Of being in the Countess of Anstruther's company more than propriety warrants. It is only because you have been forced to observe a mourning period that you have slowed down. Someday you will stand before God and account for all your deeds."

"I will stand before Him with a clear conscience."

Max raised a skeptical eyebrow, but George didn't elaborate. He couldn't. He wasn't at liberty to reveal details of his double life, even though he no longer actively worked for the Crown. There were others whose lives depended on him maintaining secrecy. One day, hopefully soon when the war ended, he'd be able to share his well-kept secret and let his brothers know he'd not forsaken their deeply held beliefs.

As it was, his cover was nearly blown four years prior in France. Navigating through thick brush by a busy road, he'd come upon an attempted ambush. By chance he'd spotted a French infantryman behind a thick hedge, waiting for two British cavalry officers riding along what should have been a safe lane.

He'd immediately recognized one of the officers as Nathan. No one sat a horse as well as he. George had slid the knife from his boot and crept through the underbrush. With deadly silence he'd dispatched the French soldier and Nathan passed by, never once suspecting how close he came to dying that day.

"I am sorry, George. I did not mean to put a damper on our evening." Max said, obviously misunderstanding his silence. As he'd done many times before, George shrugged his shoulders and behaved as though nothing bothered him. He was still the free-wheeling brother who had yet to settle down.

"No harm, Max. One day I shall find a quiet chit of a girl to marry, but not tonight."

Memories of dark curls caressing creamy shoulders and soft brown eyes gazing up at him popped into his mind. Once again Miss Catherine Bennet dared to intrude upon his thoughts. Something she'd begun to do at an alarming rate.

Although their conversation last November at Darcy's wedding breakfast lasted but a few minutes and further discussion had been rudely interrupted by the mother, he'd felt an unfamiliar quickening at the becoming blush which stained her cheeks. There was a good possibility she'd attend Nathan and Caroline's wedding at Pemberley in November where they could renew their acquaintance. That was, if she wasn't already betrothed. He rubbed his chest at the thought of another man claiming her as his own.

Max looked past George and tensed, his lips thinning with displeasure. George glanced over his shoulder to see who had elicited such a response from his unflappable brother, recognizing Lord Herbert Jacobson, the Viscount Stanhope.

"Your Grace." Viscount Stanhope acknowledged the Duke's presence.

"Stanhope," Max murmured as he walked past their table.

To George, the Viscount gave him a barely polite nod along with a slight sneer.

"He is a sorry piece of humanity," Max grumbled once Stanhope was out of hearing. "I once told Nathan he had the intelligence of a potato."

"How insulting to the potato," George quipped, grinning at the thought of Max saying aloud a less than flattering comment. "At least he was polite. Usually he calls me…" George's eyes narrowed and he twisted in his seat to watch Viscount Stanhope enter the gaming rooms.

"What does he call you?"

"…a prancing dandy."

ELIZABETH DARCY ENTERED the cozy study, arguably the smallest room at Pemberley, yet it could easily contain three of the smaller bedrooms from Longbourn. She approached her husband, busy with his ledgers and waited by the side of the desk until he glanced up.

The smile which graced his face along with the appreciative look he bestowed upon her still had the power to make her blush. She was reminded of their morning activities by the daring way he perused her body.

"Have you come to steal me away from my dusty tomes and boring ledgers?" He pushed his chair away from the desk and beckoned for her to sit on his lap, which she did with pleasure.

Once settled and a few kisses later, she lightly pushed against his chest and made him look at her properly.

"You almost make me forget what I came to discuss."

"You really did come here for something other than a kiss and a cuddle?" He attempted to steal one more kiss, but she slid from his lap and moved to place the desk firmly between them. She was more than aware Fitz would happily close and lock the door to continue this tryst, much like he did last week if she didn't give them some space. After nearly five months of marriage, the master of Pemberley's appetite for his bride hadn't abated.

"Stay at your desk, sir," she commanded in a faux haughty voice and then laughed at his glower. "Oh, Fitz, I would love nothing better than to spend the whole day with you here, but I truly do have something important to discuss and you must not distract me with all of *this*." She gave a small wave in the direction of his well-dressed body.

"Very well, Elizabeth. You will have your say and then I will have my way," he growled, adding a wolfish waggle of his eyebrows.

"Oh dear, when you begin to rhyme your words, I know I am in trouble." She settled in the comfortable chair facing the desk, smoothed her skirts and dragged in a deep breath. "I think Georgiana needs to wait one more year before she has her curtsy before the Queen."

"But—"

Elizabeth held up her hand to stop his protest.

"Hear me out before you disagree and harrumph."

"I do not harrumph. All right," he conceded at her one eyebrow arched in disbelief. "I harrumph sometimes, but why do you want her to miss another Season?"

"Several reasons. For one, she is not ready. Since our wedding her confidence has grown, with much credit being given to Caroline Bingley. Her guidance has surprisingly brought out Georgiana's desire to attempt new things, but she has lived a very sheltered life here at Pemberley. All her encounters have been with those she knows and trusts."

"What do you then propose?"

CATHERINE

"Mrs. Annesley returns next month, which is good as Georgiana misses the companionship Caroline brought, and I thought this might be a good time to invite Kitty and Mary to stay with us. Kitty is only one year older than Georgiana, and Mary a scant two years older than Kitty. I believe Mrs. Annesley would be a wonderful influence. I propose all three girls make their debut together, next year. I shall write Papa and ask that my sisters stay with us this summer."

"What you say is true, but my sister was to be presented at court this year. Aunt Matlock is thrilled to sponsor not only Georgiana, but also you, Mrs. Darcy. And, Richard will be disappointed. He looked forward to partnering his new cousin at the ball the Countess has planned."

"This brings me to my second reason to postpone Georgiana's season." She clasped her hands together, aware they'd gone damp from nerves and excitement. "As you know I have a special gown commissioned for this occasion and with such a beautiful design, I hate to ruin the cut by letting it out."

His brow furrowed. "Why on earth would you have to let it out?"

"Because, dear husband, the baby refuses to stop growing so I can be presented at court." She smiled as understanding dawned in his eyes, more than pleased she'd managed to surprise him.

"Baby?"

Those warm hazel eyes she loved so much shone bright with tears and she nodded yes. He rose from the desk and drew her to her feet, kissing her with a passion that ignited a flame in both of them.

"Your letter writing will have to wait," he whispered against her soft throat. A few hours later the door to the study was unlocked and a sleepy bride was carried to her room.

CATHERINE

Longbourn – the very next week

"Kitty?"

The halls of Longbourn echoed with the shrill sound of Mrs. Bennet on the hunt for her second youngest daughter. "Oh, where is that girl? Hill, have you seen Kitty?"

She hurried from one room to another, calling for her daughter every few seconds until Mr. Bennet cried out from his book room.

"Enough, Mrs. Bennet! Cease and desist your caterwauling. I am of a mind to banish you to your sister's house in Meryton so that I may have some peace and quiet!"

"You may well hush me, Mr. Bennet, but I have important news and cannot locate Kitty."

"I hate to ask, but I shall, otherwise I will have no peace." Mr. Bennet appeared at the door of his book room, glasses perched on the end of his nose, a book in his hand. "For what reason do you require the presence of Kitty when Mary is in the drawing room playing the pianoforte. Can she not lend you aid?"

"Oh, Mr. Bennet, you know Mary is useless in these things."

"Which can only mean you are doing something with lace and buttons. Mary, good girl that she is, abhors such frivolous activities."

"How you vex me at times with your impatience." Mrs. Bennet waved a letter in front of his face. "It so happens, Lizzy has written, inviting us to attend Pemberley this summer. We shall have to go to London and buy new clothes. I'm sure my brother has some lovely fabric in one of his warehouses."

"Let me see what Elizabeth wrote." Mr. Bennet held out his hand, his countenance showing he would brook no argument from his silly wife. With a sullen pout she handed over the letter. He raised his eyebrow when he noted the letter was addressed to him, quickly perused the pages and upon removing his glasses, said, "Get your story straight next time, Madam. Elizabeth invited Kitty and Mary to Pemberley. I see no invitation extended for you to attend with either of them."

"That's preposterous. I'm sure she wants her mama to visit and this was an oversight."

"An oversight, you say. I think not." He folded the letter and tucked it inside his book. "No, it is settled, you will say your good-byes from the front entryway and find something else to entertain yourself with while they are gone. You might even have time to visit Lady Lucas, who enjoys extolling the virtues of her new grandson, William. The one who will inherit Longbourn from his own dear father, Mr. Collins."

"Have you no regard for my nerves? Reminding me how Mr. Collins will turn me out to the hedgerows as soon as you are in the grave."

"My dear, you are completely wrong. I have the highest regard for your nerves and who knows, I may outlive you."

Chapter Three

Kitty ambled along the road between Lucas Lodge and Longbourn. She'd been visiting her very best friend, Maria Lucas and was now on her way home before the sun set and it became too dark to see the road.

Lucas Lodge was such welcome respite after the chaos that signified life at her home, Longbourn. With three of her sisters married, everyone assumed Mama would calm down and relax knowing her daughters were secure. Well, at least two of the daughters were secure. Lydia rarely wrote and when she did it was usually to petition money from 'dear mama'. As always, Mama could never say no to her 'dear girl' and much of her pin money found its way north, along with Kitty's and Mary's. Mama was not above purloining money from their treasure boxes.

This behavior should not have surprised her. Mama always favored Lydia, allowing her to take any ribbon or bonnet she fancied from her sisters, the exception being Jane. No one was permitted to take anything of Jane's.

To Kitty, Lydia's letters were filled with details of parties and balls she attended, with or without Wickham, and of flirtations with other officers. Any money being sent was not being used for food or household affairs, but for supporting a self-indulgent lifestyle. Almost a year's separation gave Kitty a more sobering view of her younger sister and what she saw filled her heart with sorrow. Nothing good could come from their degenerate lifestyle and she prayed for them daily.

She'd turned onto the road which led to Longbourn, traversing the small slope immediately following when thunderous hooves pounded from behind. Before she could move out of the way, a horse and rider crested the hill, jumping over her body at the last minute. Startled, she screamed and tumbled into the ditch.

She rolled once, arms flailing helplessly and came to a soggy stop at the bottom of the shallow gully. With shaking hands, she pushed her bonnet back off her face and took a few precious seconds to gather her wits. Nothing was broken, that she could ascertain, and her heart raced along as though she'd run all the way home from Lucas Lodge. She heard the rustling of tall grass as the rider of the horse slipped down the embankment toward her.

"Are you hurt?" he queried.

She nodded, not trusting her voice. Tears threatened to overflow onto her cheeks with the realization of how perilously close she'd come to being injured or killed.

"Here, take my hand."

She raised her hand, but when he went to pull her toward him, she cried out at the sharp pain in her side.

"You are injured!"

"I am not sure," she managed to breathe out and pressed her palm to her side where the pain still radiated.

She finally lifted her head and looked up at the rider, gasping aloud when she realized it was none other than Lord George Kerr. The last time she'd seen the handsome gentleman was at Lizzy and Jane's wedding breakfast last November. Their brief interlude had been the highlight of her whole week, ending when she'd been rudely called away by Mama.

"Miss Catherine Bennet!" He seemed equally surprised. "I am so sorry for having caused you such undue pain. Please allow me to help you up this embankment."

Her cheeks flamed with embarrassment. She'd been in raptures over the small attention received from him and for months had painted a romantic dream around his dark good looks and storm colored eyes. Now, the fantasy presented itself in living color and she was mortified to be covered in mud and weeds, through no fault of her own.

He slipped and slid closer and with a perfunctory 'Sorry', cradled her in his arms and lifted. She clenched her jaw tight and tried to not cry out but couldn't stop a small whimper from escaping.

"I am truly sorry, Miss Catherine. I would not blame your father if he called for a public flogging because of my recklessness."

"No worries, Lord Kerr," she panted out in quick breaths. "Father is not bothered by much. Mama wore him down years ago."

She thought she heard him chuckle and dared to glance up at his face, which was achingly close now that he held her in his arms. She noted a firm chin and full mouth which was most definitely curved in a smile at her comment. Before he caught her staring, like he did at Pemberley, she fixed her eyes on the ditch they were in.

"There is a natural incline over there." She pointed to the area where the gully gradually met the road. "If you must carry me, this would make it much easier to gain access. I do not wish to be a burden."

"Miss Catherine, you are no burden. I swear you are as light as a feather, but I agree, the access is much easier over there." He began walking toward the berm and within minutes set her on her feet, holding her arms for a few seconds longer until he was sure she wouldn't collapse.

"I am fine, Lord Kerr. I will be on my way." She attempted a small curtsy and winced.

"What kind of gentleman do you think I am, allowing an injured female to walk home when I have a perfectly fine horse to carry us?"

"No!" She pulled away from him and almost fell again in pain. This time, her ankle refused to hold her weight. With lightning fast reflexes, he caught her before she hit the ground. "We cannot ride together. What would people say?"

With his arms wrapped around her, he glanced up and down the road. One eyebrow arched and he grinned. "What people do you see, Miss Catherine?"

"You never know who could come along. No, I shall have to walk."

She pushed lightly against his chest and he allowed them to separate, but kept his hands firmly on her forearms, to steady her balance.

"No." His tone was resolute. "We will ride Buttons."

"Buttons?" She tried not to laugh out loud as it hurt, but the horse was a handsome steed, worthy of a name like Zeus, Juno, or Lightning.

"Laugh if you must. I bought him from a friend whose son named the beast. To change it now would confuse him greatly."

He placed his hands around her waist and lifted her with ease onto the saddle. She grimaced from the pressure on her ribs and once again he apologized. "Let us get you home and then we can send for a doctor."

With that he swung up behind her and she stiffened, arching her body away from his strong, solid one. He slid an arm around her waist, his other hand loose on the reins.

"Relax, Miss Catherine. I have you."

Jaw clenched tight, she nodded and relaxed her body into his.

"You might want to hold onto my arm, to give you better balance."

He was wedged against her so tight his voice resonated through into her body, and his essence, the sheer maleness of him surrounded her. The sensation was as much frightening as it was exciting. Face aflame, she did as he bade. All her romanticized day dreams of Lord George having his arms about her did not come close to the real thing.

Soon the thrill of his arms around her subsided. With each rocking step Button's took, pain spiraled across her ribs and it required all her concentration to take in shallow breaths.

"We are almost there, Miss Catherine. I can see a house through a break in the trees."

She lifted her gaze and almost wept at the sight of Longbourn. Both her mother and father exited the house to greet them, no doubt having been warned by a servant they were coming up the drive. She expected a full-on assault by her mother and was not disappointed.

"Whatever happened?" Mama's mouth gaped open at the sight of Kitty seated in front of Lord George, his arms around her in a familiar fashion.

He slid off the horse and turned toward Kitty. She placed her hands on his broad shoulders and with great care he lifted her off Buttons. She fully expected him to set her on her feet, instead, with little effort he swung her up into his arms and turned to face her parents.

"I apologize for this breach of decorum, but Miss Catherine has been injured. Do you have somewhere I may take her?"

"Right this way, Lord Kerr." Papa said, waving his arm in the direction of the door. He'd obviously recognized Lord George from the wedding.

"Oh, my nerves. My body is trembling. Hill, I need my smelling salts." Mama held the back of her hand to her forehead and swayed on her feet.

Mortified by her mother's antics, Kitty fought the urge to burrow her face into Lord George's shoulder. How could Mama behave so badly in front of such an esteemed guest? The son of a Duke, no less.

"Pray, calm your nerves, Mrs. Bennet." Papa paused on the doorstep and glared at his wife. "Your daughter is in need of a doctor. Kindly send a boy for him." He turned back to Lord George. "Come through to the front parlor, Lord Kerr."

Lord George followed Papa, taking care not to bump the door frames or any furniture that loomed in their path and Kitty was reminded of how gentle he'd been throughout this whole ordeal. He carried her as if she were a feather pillow and all too soon, found herself being deposited on one of the couches in the parlor.

"I must check on Buttons, Miss Catherine, and shall return shortly." Lord George stepped back and gave her a polite bow.

Kitty watched him depart, thankful that she was not standing as her legs felt as though they had the rigidity of embroidery thread. He took her breath away and if she weren't careful, her heart could become involved and that wouldn't do.

Within the hour the local doctor, Mr. Wilson attended Longbourn and treated both she and her mother. One for a bruised rib and sprained ankle, the other for a nervous disposition.

WITH HER RIBS AND ANKLE bound tight, Kitty attempted to rest on one the settees scattered about the drawing room. Lord George had stayed to dinner and as soon as it was polite, joined her. Standing by the fireplace he watched her with what she'd come to recognize as a habitual grin. Normally she would have fussed and fidgeted, but the slightest movement incurred a biting slice of pain.

"I believe you are the most fetching patient Mr. Wilson has had these past few months," Lord George offered by way of a conversation starter. "I overheard him tell your father that all he treats lately are red coated soldiers with broken noses and twisted shoulders from holding their muskets the wrong way and not learning when to duck."

"I would rather the injuries happen here than on French soil." Kitty said, thinking about the young men who would never return to Meryton. Maria Lucas worried constantly about her brother, Jonathan. They hadn't heard from him in over a month.

At one time, Kitty fancied herself in love with the tall, lanky boy. Not hard to do when they were such close neighbors, but he never saw her in the same light. Over time and a few shed tears, she learned to treasure their friendship and when he'd enlisted, added him to her daily prayers along with Lydia, Elizabeth, Jane and Georgiana.

"There are many in France who live for the day that *'Le Corse'* is defeated," Lord George muttered, the muscles along his jawline clenching as his lips formed a thin line.

There were bitter tones laced throughout that one short statement and she was filled with curiosity at his brief display of emotion.

"You sound as though you have been there and seen that for yourself."

If she hadn't been watching him so closely, she wouldn't have seen him give a small start. Minutiae in terms of reactions, but there all the same.

"No, not this boring English gentleman. My French is deplorable, almost as bad as my Latin." He pretended to shudder. "I took an interest in what Old Boney was up to when Nathan enlisted. I played no part in the war."

A revised quote from Shakespeare fluttered through her mind at his declaration.

The gentleman doth protest too much, methinks.

Kitty determined Lord George didn't want her to question his connection with France and nervously pleated the throw rug on her lap. She wondered how much longer her family would take before they joined them. Although she was infirm and Lord George was clear across the room by the fireplace, the fact they were alone in the drawing room was socially unacceptable.

As if on cue, Mary entered the room and sat opposite her, Mama and Papa not far behind.

GEORGE WATCHED WITH mild amusement as Mrs. Bennet fussed with her skirts, chastised her daughters for any number of things not worth worrying about and almost laughed out loud when she finally turned her full attention toward him. The calculated gleam in her eye, barely concealed by much fluttering of eyelashes, led him to believe she'd pegged him as son-in-law number four.

"We barely had time for conversation, what with all the excitement of Kitty nearly being killed."

George caught a slight eye roll from Catherine, who hid it by looking down at her fingers, which continued to pleat and tug at the blanket covering her legs. If she kept that up, the poor thing would be torn to shreds before night's end.

"What brought you to Hertfordshire, Lord Kerr? Surely there are lots of pretty girls in London to catch your eye, although Kitty is quite lovely when she's not covered in mud."

Mrs. Bennet's head tipped to one side as she waited for an answer. She reminded him of a pet bird his mother kept, which always tilted its head and fixed one eye on him, waiting to see what he'd say or do.

"Mrs. Bennet, Lord Kerr is not required to share his itinerary, nor does he answer to us as to what ladies he knows in London." Mr. Bennet shook out his newspaper in agitation. "It is not his fault Kitty was in the middle of the road. Silly girl, always day dreaming her life away."

George noted a tightening of Catherine's lips and a faint blush staining her cheeks, the only visible clue that her parent's behavior shamed her deeply and he felt a tug of compassion. For some reason he felt an insane desire to spirit her away so they could never embarrass her this way again, but for now he placed the well-worn cloak of a shallow man around his shoulders and waded into the inane world of Mrs. Bennet.

"I do not mind answering Mrs. Bennet's questions and it is not Miss Catherine's fault for her accident. I was in a mad rush to deliver a letter."

"What? The post does not run from London anymore?" Mr. Bennet dropped the top half of his paper down and looked at George in mock astonishment.

George revised his opinion of the couple. Although Mrs. Bennet was shallow and rather empty-headed, Mr. Bennet was an observer of people. He'd have to tread carefully around the man.

"Yes, it does, but a friend of mind, Lord Alvanley placed a bet that I would be unable deliver the letter to a mutual friend's door in less than twelve hours. Alas, I now owe him ten pounds."

"Ten pounds!" Mrs. Bennet gasped out loud, her hand fluttering up to her chest. "You must have a great deal of money if you can bet such exorbitant amounts."

If only he were in this part of England for such a whimsical reason. While Mrs. Bennet nattered on about placing bets and how she'd heard that some of the men in the village were known to play cards for money, George mulled over the true reason he was in the vicinity of Hertfordshire.

After his encounter with Stanhope at White's, he remembered where he'd seen Reggie before. He was none other than the Viscount's valet, a weasel faced character always found in areas where servants didn't congregate. Upon this realization, a few details fell into place, such as the surprised expression on Reggie's face when he first entered the parlor at Lady Evangeline's home. George remained convinced his presence was not expected and because Reggie conveniently died with this information, there was a good possibility Stanhope remained in the dark about George's covert activities.

Then again, Stanhope might not be involved at all. Servants heard and saw the underbelly of London Society and a cunning servant could use certain information to upgrade their station in life. However, George remained convinced the valet was not one to willingly get his hands dirty, which led him back to taking a closer look at the Viscount.

He planned to reconnoiter Stanhope's estate, Creighton Castle, and see if there was anything other than a very dead valet pointing to his involvement with the French. Running over a beautiful young woman on the road was not part of the plan. With that one small diversion, his hope of remaining incognito had gone up in a plume of lavender scented smoke. Once he gathered more information and or any damning evidence, he'd approach Lord Grayson with his findings.

George cursed his bad luck of literally running into Miss Catherine Bennet, not that he wasn't pleased to see her again. Except now that he'd crossed the threshold of the Bennet residence with their daughter in his arms, the whole of Meryton would soon know he'd been in the vicinity. He'd been forced to come up with an alibi of delivering a letter to a friend in Cambridge. Fortunately, Mrs. Bennet by her inquisitive nature unknowingly aided him in expounding the untruth.

"How long will you be staying in Meryton, Lord Kerr?" Mrs. Bennet asked, having exhausted her repertoire of gambling men in Meryton. She picked up a piece of embroidery stretched around a hoop. Mr. Bennet, newspaper now completely abandoned, watched him with great intent.

"I will take a room at the inn and continue my journey on the morrow."

"Oh no, you must stay here. I insist. It would be most unchristian of us to send you out in the dark of night." She dropped the hoop on the small table and clapped her hands. "Mary."

Mary, the quiet sister whom George had forgotten was in the room, lifted her head from the book she was reading. She looked at her mother, her expression evident she had not followed any portion of their discussion. He found himself fascinated by her singular devotion to exclude herself from their activities. Did Miss Bennet not care that she'd been summoned like a common servant, or worse, a household pet?

"Yes, mama?"

"Find Hill and have her prepare Jane's old room for Lord Kerr."

Miss Bennet rose in silence and started for the door.

"No thank you, Mrs. Bennet," George stated. "I am perfectly content taking a room at the inn."

Mrs. Bennet started to insist, but her husband interrupted her.

"I am sure Lord Kerr does not wish to stay in a house full of silly girls, Mrs. Bennet," he offered, clearly wishing to agitate his wife further. For once, she refused to take the bait, just huffed out a sigh and pursed her lips.

"Truly, I cannot tread upon your hospitality any longer, Mrs. Bennet." George softened his answer with what he hoped was a winsome smile.

Miss Bennet halted by the door and glanced toward her mother for direction.

"Oh, do sit down, Mary. You're not needed now." Mrs. Bennet scowled and waved her hand in the direction of the chair her daughter had previously occupied.

Internally, George winced at the manner with which Catherine's mother dismissed her middle daughter, who moved back to her chair in the corner and picked up an extremely thick book. Without so much as a flounce of her skirt, or a single flirtatious look, she began reading. Strange girl, he thought. She possessed pleasant enough features, when her mouth wasn't so downturned. In fact, she favored her elder sister, Elizabeth quite a bit. Both had dark hair and eyes and he was now convinced that if Miss Bennet were discussing something of interest, her eyes would sparkle much like Mrs. Darcy's.

"Will you be passing through Hertfordshire on your return trip to London?" Mrs. Bennet's hopeful tone broke into his thoughts and almost made him laugh. Although a rather vulgar woman by Society's standards, she couldn't be faulted for looking after her daughter's best interest. Poor woman, she didn't have to try so hard. He already was attracted to Catherine Bennet; however, he would not grant her mother the pleasure of that knowledge.

He glanced over to where Catherine lay, noting her pallor and slumped shoulders. It was apparent that her pain had not yet abated and he wondered if he had any laudanum in his saddle bag to give her. Having cracked his ribs once or twice after falling off his horse, George knew the discomfort she must be enduring. Yet not one word of complaint had passed her lips. He cut a glance at the mother, who more than made up for Catherine's silence.

"Once my obligation has concluded, I shall stop in briefly at my estate in Cambridgeshire before returning. I have not been there in almost seven years."

"You do not live on your estate? How do you know your steward is not robbing you blind?" Mr. Bennet asked in clear astonishment.

George immediately regretted mentioning the estate he would inherit from his mother. His concern for Catherine Bennet was distracting him and she hadn't so much as smiled at him. If Nathan or Max knew how much she befuddled him, they'd laugh so hard, tears would fall. He'd always been the one who showed no emotion when it came to young misses. In fact, he avoided them like the plague. He'd managed to avoid determined mama's and their insipid charges for over seven years. Yet – this quiet slip of a girl had him in a dither.

"You are a good friend, to do this task of delivering a letter, Lord Kerr." Catherine spoke up for the first time.

George felt a pinch of regret at the outright lies he spewed, but for King and country he'd done worse. The Bennet's must never know the true reason for his trip. Stanhope was an unknown threat at this time and he didn't want to cast any shadows upon them. The less they knew, the safer they'd be.

"Thank you, Miss Catherine, but I enjoyed the thrill of winning the bet more than the satisfaction of having done a good deed." He afforded her a sly wink only she could see. "Besides, it allowed me to spend time with you and your delightful family."

She blushed again and cast her gaze down to her lap. He quickly shifted his attention back to Mrs. Bennet, so as not to bring censure onto Catherine, but not before he caught a hint of a smile tilting the corner of her full, soft lips.

"By the time you return, Kitty will be leaving for London," Mrs. Bennet complained, a small whine tinging her voice. "She is to spend Easter with her Aunt and Uncle Gardiner before repairing to Derbyshire for the summer. Her sister, Mrs. Darcy, has invited her and Mary to stay until your brother's wedding at Pemberley."

"What day are you traveling to London, Miss Catherine?" George addressed his question to Catherine, hoping to draw her into the conversation once more.

"I was to leave two days hence, but Mr. Wilson advised I must wait at least a week to allow the rib to heal."

"Allow me to escort Miss Catherine to her Aunt Gardiner's." George turned to Mr. Bennet. "As I am responsible for her injuries, I feel impelled to make sure she arrives safe and sound."

"Oh, that would be most gracious of you, Lord Kerr. So magnanimous of you to offer. Isn't that so, Mr. Bennet?" Mrs. Bennet waved her hands in front of her skirts, as though she didn't know what to do with them.

"Most magnanimous, my dear." Mr. Bennet agreed, his tone rich with irony.

For all his strange quirks and seemingly uncaring attitude toward his daughters, as George had seen exhibited at Darcy's wedding breakfast, Mr. Bennet had obviously decided to watch his remaining two daughters with more caution. For that reason, he addressed the father with a humbler attitude.

"I would never forgive myself if Miss Catherine were unable to visit her family in London because of my carelessness." He patted his inside coat pocket, where he'd stuffed some folded blank papers. "I have only to deliver these letters to my friend and then I shall return to join Miss Catherine a week from tomorrow."

George knew if he left early enough, he'd make his mother's estate in Cambridgeshire by late afternoon, where he'd change into laborer's clothing and scout out Stanhope's estate a few short miles away. George had not been in the area for a long time and with careful disguise no one of consequence should recognize him as the son of the former Lady Margaret Knox, now the Dowager Duchess of Adborough. He estimated at least five days of scouting around before he had to return to Longbourn.

Mr. Bennet placed his newspaper on a small side table, rose from his chair and stopped beside George.

"A word, if I may, Lord Kerr?"

George rose to his feet and gave a polite nod to the ladies before following Mr. Bennet to his book room. Once they were seated and Mr. Bennet had poured them each a snifter of brandy, he turned his astute gaze upon George.

"My wife and daughters may believe your well contrived story of 'delivering a letter' to a friend, but I am afraid I see past your façade and demand to know what you are doing here."

Surprised by the ease at which Mr. Bennet had correctly assessed his character, George took his time in answering. Although he no longer actively worked for Lord Grayson, anything he shared held the potential of serious, if not fatal, repercussions. Bennet's connections and loyalty were an unknown factor and as such, he could not answer him with complete truthfulness.

"As I stated, I am taking a letter to—"

"I never thought of myself as a stupid man. I am sure I do not look like a stupid man, yet you continue to treat me as one." Mr. Bennet's eyes narrowed as he pinned his intelligent gaze on George. "Do you think of me as deranged, Lord Kerr?"

Clearly, he was not going to sidestep the issue with Miss Catherine's father. He placed his snifter on a small table and leaned forward.

"Mr. Bennet, I can tell you in all honesty, your daughter is not in any danger from me. My reason's for traveling to Cambridgeshire are not mine to share."

Mr. Bennet stroked his chin, deep in thought. After a few minutes, never removing his gaze from George, he replied.

"I trust you Lord Kerr and that speaks highly of you. Sadly, I have learned that scoundrels come in many forms, some of them in the guise of an officer and a gentleman, others sporting a title with no goodness in their heart. Having said that, I believe you speak the truth. I intend to reflect on your words and actions and when you return, seven days hence, I shall let you know if you may escort my daughter to London."

"Thank you, sir. I believe we could become good friends and insist you call me Lord George. With two brothers, it becomes confusing as to which Lord Kerr people are talking about." He rose to his feet and gave Mr. Bennet a polite bow. "Please bid your wife and daughters goodnight. I leave at first light and need to attain a room at the inn."

"I am not against you staying here at Longbourn."

"You and I both know that would not be advisable. I have a reputation that precedes me and if I were to spend even one night under your roof, your neighbors would speculate about your daughter's virtue. No, I must get a room at Meryton."

"If that were true, what of her virtue, should she travel alone with you to London?"

George felt the corner of his mouth lift. "Then you must ensure she has a chaperone. Her sister may enjoy a visit to London. Think how quiet your house will be."

"You are a cagey fellow, Lord George." Mr. Bennet laughed out loud. "I may learn to like you. Yes, Mary will attend London with Kitty. She needs to expand her horizon beyond Fordyce's Sermons."

Chapter Four

Kitty awoke the next morning to the rolling sound of thunder, stretched her arms over her head and cried out with pain. Although Mr. Wilson warned she'd have stiffness and feel somewhat the worse today, she'd held onto a faint hope that he'd exaggerated in an effort to make her rest longer.

No worries there. Her ankle throbbed and her side felt as though their horse had kicked her. She managed to sit on the edge of her bed and raised her nightgown. A dark blotch of deep purple and black blossomed down her right side and a quick glance at her ankle showed it to be still swollen, although not as badly bruised as her rib cage.

Rain battered against the window and her thoughts flew to Lord George. He would become soaked to the bone riding to Cambridgeshire. Maybe he'd delay his journey and pay them another courtesy visit. Her musings were interrupted by a gentle knock at the door and Mary poked her head around the corner, her eyes widening at the sight of Kitty's bruised side.

"That looks perfectly dreadful." She pushed the door open with her shoulder and advanced into the room carrying a tray with some tea and scones. "I brought you something to eat as I was sure you wouldn't be able to join us downstairs. Mr. Wilson was quite perturbed when he heard you'd stayed downstairs last night and had dinner with us all."

"Mr. Wilson saw me in my night clothes?" Kitty gasped, horrified the good doctor may have entered the room to examine her and she hadn't awakened.

"No, when he heard you were still resting he stayed briefly to chat with Papa and assured us, and more to the point, assured Mama that rest was the best medicine before continuing on his way. He is a very practical man which is probably why Mama detests him."

Kitty's shoulders slumped in relief. For a moment she worried the laudanum Lord Kerr added to her tea last night worked better than expected and she'd slept through the doctor's examination. She must remember to thank him when he returned, for if it weren't for her aching side and throbbing ankle, she felt most refreshed.

Mary set down the tray and turned to leave.

"Mary. Stay and have tea with me."

"Are you sure?"

"We are sisters, are we not? All we have is each other now our siblings are married and moved away. I would like to think we can find common ground."

A small smile lit up her sister's normally resolute features and Kitty was glad she'd asked her to stay.

"I shall fetch another cup and be right back." Mary turned to leave.

"Would you ask Cook if she can spare some strawberry preserve? I know how much you like that."

"I will see what I can do."

Kitty settled against the pillows and while waiting for her sister, turned her thoughts toward the enigmatic Lord George. He perplexed her greatly. One minute she perceived great intellect, similar to Elizabeth and Darcy and then, like a coin turning over, he played the foppish fool. What was he hiding? Better yet, whom was he hiding from? The question played around the edges of her brain until Mary returned with a small bowl of preserves in one hand and an empty tea cup in the other.

Within minutes both of them were enjoying their tea and a scone. Kitty couldn't remember a time when she and Mary simply sat together, other than at church. In some ways, both of them were overlooked. Jane was the beautiful sister, Elizabeth the wit, and Lydia the favorite. When all five sisters lived within the walls of Longbourn, she and Mary had been afterthoughts to most people.

She'd been the silly sister who followed Lydia in all things and Mary always behaved in a most pious manner, putting a damper on most of their activities. Well, not her activities per se. Mostly Lydia's, which Kitty had happily engaged in until... well, until George Wickham entered their lives like a wild winter snowstorm.

Once Lydia met him she became even more untamable. None of the family knew how many times she'd snuck out to meet him. Kitty had begged her to behave in a more circumspect manner until Lydia resorted to teasing, saying she was becoming 'just like Mary'. Angry and hurt that her closest sister was abandoning her in favor of a man, she'd retorted she'd never be like Mary.

Cruel words and not for the first time she'd had to ask forgiveness for thinking such unchristian like thoughts toward her own sister. A sister who didn't deserve her anger or uncalled for criticism.

"I am so glad we have this moment of peace together." Impulsively, she reached out and grabbed Mary's hand. "At times I feel we are strangers living under the same roof."

Clearly surprised, Mary withdrew her hand and sipped her tea. Kitty worried she'd offended her elder sister. About to apologize, she stopped when Mary spoke in a soft voice.

"I too am glad for this moment of respite. We do not get very many of them in our house, what with Mama and all her nervous fluttering."

"Mary! I think that is the most uncharitable thing you've ever said," she teased with a small laugh. Mary's smile faltered and she grabbed her sister's hand again. "I am not censuring you. I happen to agree with you. Our parents are intractable."

"Recalcitrant."

"Pertinacious."

Both girls giggled, the warmest sounds of sisterly affection the walls of Longbourn had heard in a great while. In time their laughter ceased although the good will lingered.

"Papa would be quite pleased at our grasp of the English language, but I for one do not wish him to know I read quite extensively. As long as he thinks I am the silliest girl in all of England, he leaves me alone." Kitty took a tiny bite of her scone.

"Papa would be surprised to know how many books I have borrowed from the lending library. I am particularly fond of Mrs. Ann Radcliffe."

"You have read *The Mysteries of Udolpho*?" Kitty couldn't hide the surprise in her voice.

"Yes, and Lord Byron."

"How can Papa and Mama not know of this?"

"Why do you think I cart Fordyce's Sermons with me wherever I go?"

"What does Fordyce's Sermons have to do with you reading *The Mysteries of Udolpho*?"

"Can you keep a secret?"

"You are talking to the sister who single handily kept Lydia's assignations with Wickham in Meryton quiet for months."

"There is that. Not a shining example, but I trust you." Mary stood. "I shall be right back."

What in the world was Mary up to, and what did it have to do with the boring tome of *Fordyce's Sermons to Young Women*. Oh no. Did she intend to read from the voluminous book?

Forgive me Lord, but I really, really do not want a sermon this early in the morning.

Mary slipped back into the room with the Fordyce's thick volume cradled in her arms. Kitty placed her cup and empty plate on the nightstand by her bed, then shifted – with only one small wince – to make room for her sister. Mary quickly sat on the edge of the counterpane and with a furtive glance toward the door, opened the book.

At first Kitty could only stare in astonishment. The book had been hollowed out and nestled within lay a novel borrowed from the lending library.

"Mary, you are a genius." She began to laugh and then had to stop as pain sliced through her side. "Oh, laughing hurts, and that is too bad because this is worthy of a good chuckle."

"You won't tell Mama and Papa?"

"Never. However, if I get the chance, may I share this with Lizzy and Jane?"

"Let me think on that. I am not willing to shed my dour personality just yet."

"Regardless, your secret is safe with me."

Marveled at how much she enjoyed Mary's company, Kitty spent the next half hour talking about books and music with a sister who before had been more of a stranger than family. Their visit was brought short by the call of their mother, looking for Mary.

"It seems since you are indisposed, I am the one she has to rely on." Mary quietly gathered their dishes onto the tray. Before opening the door, she turned to face Kitty. "I am very glad you weren't more seriously hurt. I do not know what I will do when I am the only sister left at Longbourn."

"I am not going anywhere for a long time. There are no eligible men in Hertfordshire and you know that when we visit Aunt and Uncle Gardiner in London, we will never visit families who have marriage minded sons."

Mary lifted an eyebrow at Kitty's impassioned statement.

"There may be no eligible men in Meryton, but there is definitely a man interested in you Catherine Eleanor Bennet. Lord George Kerr." With that she opened the door and left to find their mother.

Kitty lay back on her pillows and fixed her gaze on the rivulets of water trickling down her window pane. Dare she hope that a dashing gentleman, a noble man to be exact, held some regard for her.

Stuff and nonsense. She was gently bred, but his family would never tolerate the second son of a Duke to marry a girl with such low connections, even if she were a gentleman's daughter. They would expect him to marry a Lady. Someone whose family was great and ancient.

Her heart pinched a little at the thought she'd never stand a chance with the dashing rogue. Even if he did ask to court her, she'd have to decline. Once he knew her secret he'd never wish to speak with her again. No, she would die a spinster and he would find a lovely young lady of quality to be his bride.

How lucky that woman would be. Life with him would be exciting, of that she was sure and hoped whoever he chose for a bride was up for the adventure.

GEORGE URGED BUTTONS on. The rain had not let up since they'd departed the inn early that morning, but with his mother's estate only a few miles away it seemed such a shame to stop now. Besides, one couldn't get any wetter than the two of them were right at that moment. They passed beneath a large tree and a cascade of rainwater poured off the branches. Rivers of ice cold liquid sluiced past his collar and swept down his back. He revised his previous thought. He could become wetter.

"Just a few more miles, Buttons. I promise some dry oats and a nice blanket to keep you warm." He patted the horse's neck, which shook out his mane by way of reply, spraying George's face with even more moisture.

"I guess I deserved that, making you plod along muddy side roads. I know you like the more traveled path, but I could not take the chance of anyone recognizing me." He looked around at the surrounding fields, turning a verdant green from the much-needed watering. Given the severity of the storm, he probably could have taken the main road. Only a fool, or an ex-spy on a mission, would be out and about in this foul weather.

He'd much rather be back at Longbourn, teasing the pretty Miss Catherine. He thought back to their short ride yesterday. At first, she'd held herself stiff, fighting the pain from her ribs, but at his urging she allowed herself to rest against his chest and he'd found the experience satisfying. It was as though she belonged there, next to his heart.

He couldn't stop from smiling at the irony of his situation. So many ambitious young ladies attempted to catch his interest, willing to disregard his unwarranted reputation as a rogue, all for the chance of being related to a Duke. Notwithstanding that if anything happened to his brother, Maxwell, he'd be the sixth Duke of Adborough.

All their arts and allurements were for naught, as an unassuming miss from the middle of Hertfordshire might claim the prize as her own. He recalled how trim her waist felt when he lifted her onto Buttons and even though covered by mud and weeds, her skin carried a light scent of lavender. If not for her injuries, he'd have made the ride last a little longer just so he could hold her in his arms.

Finally, he reached the road leading to his mother's estate, Keswick Manor. Buttons nickered at the familiar terrain.

"There she is, boy. One more mile and then—"

With an agitated whinny, Buttons suddenly reared, unseating George who promptly landed in the ditch filled with water. He fully expected the horse to bolt, but all his patient training kept the handsome steed close, albeit a little skittish by whatever spooked him.

George pulled himself from the water and scrambled onto the road, snagging Buttons' halter in case he changed his mind and decided to make a break for Keswick Manor.

"What is it, boy? What has got you all fired up?" He spoke in a soothing voice and ran an experienced hand over the horse's flesh, checking to make sure there wasn't some unseen injury. He paused when his fingers ran across a small welt on Buttons' right hind quarters. At that exact moment he felt a sharp sting on his neck.

"What the...?"

His hand flew up to swat whatever had bit him. Within his peripheral vision he caught sight of a boy, seated in a tree by the side of the road. He pretended he hadn't seen the little blighter and spoke to the horse in a louder than normal voice.

"Well, there must be some wasps out now that the rain has stopped. I hope they don't interfere with my digging for gold."

As he suspected, the boy lowered the device he'd used to sling tiny rocks, clearly intrigued by the thought of gold. Thank goodness it hadn't been anything more sinister. His mental musings about Miss Catherine had dulled his senses. Had this been France, he'd be dead.

He swung up into the saddle and flicked the reins. Buttons obliged by moving off at a slow walk. Now that he was aware of the child, George clearly heard him clambering out of the tree and trying to follow in the rain-soaked underbrush. The boy was going to become very wet.

Good.

George continued past the drive to Keswick Manor and headed for the small house where their groundskeeper took lodging. He stopped in front of a small barn, slid off Buttons and tied him to a post. He then strode around to the back of the house and waited for the lad. He didn't have to wait long. No more than five minutes passed before he heard shuffling behind the stone fence that encircled the small yard and garden.

When he judged the boy was passing by his location, he stood and with a quick hand reached over the low fence and grabbed him by the shirt collar.

"Oi. Wot do you want wif me?"

The grimy faced urchin kicked and wiggled in vain.

"I would like to know why you attempted to injure my horse."

"I dunno wot yer yabberin' about."

George hauled the boy over the fence and plunked him down, keeping a firm hand on his neck.

"You launched a rock and hit my horse on his flank, which I know you thought was funny as I fell arse over tea kettle," – the boy sniggered – "but what if the horse landed into a rut and broke his leg."

"I never thought of that." The boy stopped struggling and lowered his head. "Wot you gonna do wif me?"

George paused and thought about his options. By the amount of filth encrusted on the child there was a good chance he didn't have caring parents. Or at least parents who could afford to keep their children clean. He seemed slightly malnourished, given how George could feel fragile bones through the threadbare shirt.

No, the punishment had to be fitting, yet fair.

"What is your name?"

"Phillip." The boy dared to glance up at George.

"That is a good strong name. One you can live up to." George glanced toward Keswick Manor. "I have a task you can do which is quite fitting for the crime."

At the word 'crime' the boy began to squirm again. George tightened his grip, trying not to bruise the frail child. "Settle down, Phillip. I am not turning you over to the magistrate."

The young lad stopped struggling.

"Seeing as you nearly caused irreparable harm to my horse, I believe I shall have you water, feed and care for him while I'm here in Cambridgeshire."

"I cain't feed yer 'orse. Ain't got no money fer that."

"I shall provide everything you require. Your job is to take care of Buttons."

"Buttons?"

Phillip grinned, showing a gap between some of his teeth, which made George think he was only about eight or nine years old. At least that was how old he'd been when all he had to show for a smile was his two front teeth and nothing on either side.

"Yes, my horse's name is Buttons. Are we in accord you will look after him?"

"I dunno. I'm supposed to help me mum and there ain't no pay lookin after yer 'orse."

What a sad state of affairs that a child had to worry about bringing money home for the family.

"What would you say if I paid you a half guinea for a job well done."

"A half guinea?" Phillip squeaked out, his eyes wide.

"For a job well done," George stressed. "You must do a good job in order to receive the full amount."

He already knew he'd pay the boy a half guinea even if the job was incomplete, but Phillip didn't need to know that.

"I can help you hunt fer gold."

George had to swallow a laugh. He'd forgotten about mentioning gold, clearly Phillip had not. Smart lad.

"I am not here for gold. That was a ruse to entice you behind the house."

"You talk pretty fancy fer a git."

George crouched down so he could look Phillip face to face.

"Take care how you speak to me, Master Phillip. This 'git' is the one who will pay you a good wage for honest labor." Assured he had Phillip's complete attention, he rose to his feet. "We shall settle Buttons and then you can commence with the job at hand."

He'd decided to sleep in the rooms above the stable for the duration of his stay. The head groomsmen, Mr. Bryant wouldn't tell a soul who he really was and he could pose as his nephew. There was too much risk of being seen and recognized trying to enter and leave Keswick Manor.

"Fer 'ow long?" Phillip asked as they turned in the direction of the stable.

"I shall be here for a week. I have not seen my uncle for a few years and we have much to discuss."

"Yer Mr. Bryant's nephew?"

"Aye." George slipped into a Yorkshire slang. It wouldn't do for a common laborer to talk like a Duke's well-educated son.

"I never knew 'e had family."

"Ye know most people 'round 'ere, doncha Phillip."

"Aye. Me mum works for Viscount Stanhope and sees all sorts of grand people."

"She does? What about your father?" he managed to ask in a calm voice. His mind raced with various scenarios at the mention of Stanhope. He could use Phillip to gain entrance to the manor, or maybe his mother might impart secrets. The possibilities were endless.

"Me da is dead."

They'd reached Buttons and Phillip, without being asked, untied the reins and began leading the horse toward the stable. George was impressed by the way this young boy instinctively knew what to do and do it well. If Phillip continued in this vein, he'd speak with Mr. Bryant and see if the boy could do small jobs to supplement the family's income.

"Who stays with you? If your ma works at Creighton Castle, she must live there."

Phillip hunched his shoulders, his head hanging low and George knew the answer. His heart tightened at the thought of this young boy fending for himself. Not saying another word, he followed Phillip into the stable and directed him to an empty stall.

"There's some oats in the bag over there, take this pail and fill it while I remove the saddle."

He'd slung the saddle over a bench and was in the process of removing the blanket by the time Phillip returned. The boy held the pail for Buttons, gently stroking his forelock. George watched him in contemplative silence and decided to try a different tac.

"Do I need to worry you'll abandon me 'orse to take care of things at 'ome? I know what it's like t'have brothers and sisters depend on you."

"Only got one sister." Phillip kept his head down.

"Good on ya then. Someone who can cook and take care of the house."

"Sally cain't cook."

"What? How does she expect to marry and have children of her own?"

"She's only four."

"Four!"

Phillip dropped the pail and made to run. George snagged him by the midsection and held tight as once again the lad squirmed and wiggled. Buttons danced away from the two of them, then lowered his head and ate the remaining oats out of the pail, unaided.

"Stop this at once! I will not harm you."

The boy stopped wriggling. A weight of sadness settled about George's shoulders at the realization of how much responsibility lay on this young lad. He set Phillip on his feet and with gentle hands, turned him around.

"Take me to your sister."

"Cain't do that."

"And why not?" George felt a niggling headache begin behind his eyes at the introduction of another delay. This day was not going forward as planned. He was soaked to the bone, standing in the stable of his mother's estate, arguing with an intractable child.

"Me mum gave 'er to Mrs. Puddicombe, 'cuz she threatened to call the magistrate."

"Phillip, I am sorry. Where do you stay?"

"'Ere and there."

George had a sneaking suspicion 'here and there' was any place which sheltered him from the rain or snow.

"Does Mrs. Puddicombe take care of you as well?"

"Nah, Mrs. Puddicombe says me mum can only afford to send money for Sally." Phillip stood as tall as he could and looked George straight in the eye. "I can look after meself and when I'm old enough, I'm going to take Sally away from 'ere."

For a moment, George met his defiant stare and then nodded.

"I believe you. Come, let's get Buttons bedded down. You start your job first thing in the morning."

He handed Phillip a brush and showed him how to groom a horse properly. While the boy was busy with his new task, George headed for the second floor and checked out the state of the rooms. All of them had comfortable iron beds with a minimum of furniture. There was a time when every room housed a junior groomsman, but with his mother residing at Adborough Hall, there was no need for the extra staff.

Descending the stairs, he heard Mr. Bryant.

"You, boy. What are you doing with 'is Lordship's 'orse?"

George bounded down the stairs and answered before Phillip could speak.

"Uncle John. How are you?"

Mr. Bryant froze, uncertainty marring his rugged face. At George's sly wink, he gave a wide smile.

"I'm doin' grand."

"Phillip, I placed some blankets on one of the beds upstairs. Go on and make your bed and then come back down for something to eat."

The boy headed up the stairs and George indicated with a nod for Mr. Bryant to follow him out to the back paddock. Once safely out of Phillip's hearing, he explained the need to pose as his nephew.

"I'll do whatever you need, M'Lord. I guess I should tell my Anna there's two more for supper."

"Thank you, Mr. Bryant. I think you will find Phillip to be a quick study and I am sure he will be a good junior groomsman in no time."

"Not many 'orses 'ere to groom these days, what with the Duchess gone t'the North."

George turned and took in the view of Keswick Manor's grounds and buildings. Maybe it was time he took up his mother's offer to sign the estate over to him. He'd declined before because he'd been knee deep in espionage, but now that he'd 'retired', the estate could use his attention.

"Mr. Bryant, my mother has offered me Keswick Manor, and I believe I shall accept. It is time we bring this place back to life."

Chapter Five

With her head resting against the back of the settee, Kitty fought to keep her eyes open. Aunt Philips was seated across from their mother, their tea gone cold they'd been gossiping for so long. Mama insisted Kitty stay downstairs until after supper, but she was exhausted. Her sleep remained disturbed every time she moved in the bed.

Fortunately, the pain from her ribs had decreased dramatically to a dull ache and by the end of the week, when Lord George returned, she planned on being fit to travel. Two days hence, Mr. Wilson promised to check her progress and advise Papa. She'd even walk upright and bear the pain to sway the good doctor's opinion. Nothing would keep her from attending Aunt and Uncle Gardiner's home in London. This was her first time being invited and it was long overdue.

Mama and Aunt Philips had spoken of nothing else but Lord George from the minute Aunt walked through the door. How much more could they expound upon his features, his clothing, his manners? After a polite half hour Papa scuttled back to his book room and Mary took to practicing the pianoforte in the other parlor.

Kitty cocked her head and listened. The music sounded beautiful, almost haunting in its rendering. She closed her eyes and let the perfectly executed melody flow through her senses. No longer did she wince when her elder sister pounded the ivory keys. It seemed her elder sister held more than secret books close to her chest. She hoped that were true. Mary suffered enough of Mama's thoughtless tongue. Why, at one Assembly, she had declared that Mary couldn't carry a tune, even if she put the music in a bucket and walked around with it.

"Oh sister, he had such an air about him, such a gentleman and he must have a vast fortune. He thought nothing of losing ten pounds. Ten pounds! Can you imagine?"

"No, indeed I could not."

"And that's not all. He made sure our Kitty was looked after. He even gave us some of his own laudanum so she would rest easy."

"Truly a gentleman. We don't have many of them here, in Meryton."

"No, we do not. Lady Lucas would like us to believe her family's all high and mighty, but I remember her from before Sir William was knighted." Mama shook out her skirt in agitation. "She didn't have Lucas Lodge back then and it's not nearly as grand as Longbourn."

"Now, Fanny. Don't get upset. Everyone knows you are the better hostess. People vie for invitations to your dinners."

"Yes, they do." Mollified, Mama settled back and fanned her cheeks. "And my girls have married well. No paltry vicars for them. My Jane and Lizzy are mistresses of grand estates and Lydia is the belle of the ball in Newcastle – wherever that is." Mama glanced over to her injured daughter. "And Kitty's on her way to a great marriage as well. Lord Kerr is besotted. Why, he had his arms around her in a most forward manner. I'm surprised Mr. Bennet didn't have the banns read this past Sunday over his behavior."

"Mama!" Kitty protested. "Lord George had no choice but to hold me on the horse or I would have fallen off. There was nothing untoward in his behavior at all."

She couldn't stop the heat from rising upon her cheeks at the memory of his strong arms, or how wonderful it had felt to lean back against his solid chest. For a moment she wondered what it would be like to always have him there, making sure she was protected.

She shook her head. Never going to happen and it was time she pulled her thoughts out of the clouds and prepare to be more ladylike and act with understated decorum when he escorted her and Mary to London.

"I've watched many men throughout my life Catherine Bennet and I know when a man is more than interested in a young woman." Mama turned to face her sister. "You mark my words. Lord George Kerr will ask Mr. Bennet if he can pay his addresses before the month is out."

"You're never wrong, Fanny. Look at Bingley. It took him an inordinate amount of time to ask for Jane's hand, but you had him pegged right from the start."

"Yes, I did." Mama preened. She loved to be in the right and her sister loved to stroke her ego. "I knew she couldn't be so beautiful for nothing."

Mary entered the room and moved to sit with Kitty. Before she settled, and while her back was to their mother and aunt, she rolled her eyes. Kitty stifled a giggle for two reasons. One, her ribs still ached and two, her mother didn't require more reason to believe that she was a silly girl.

"I heard you playing, Mary. Were you trying out a new piece?" she asked.

Mary carefully arranged her skirts before answering. "Yes. I was inspired by Miss Darcy's playing when we were last at Pemberley and asked Papa if I could purchase some sheets of Mozart's music."

"Whatever you chose was beautiful. I quite liked it."

"Thank you," Mary said, her cheeks flushing a becoming pink.

All the ladies' attention was drawn to the door of the parlor when their butler appeared.

"Mrs. Bingley," Griggs announced.

"Jane has come!" Mama rose to her feet and hurried to the door, greeting her eldest daughter with a kiss on the cheek. She glanced over Jane's shoulder toward the front entry. "Is Charles not with you, dear?"

"No, Mama. We have only just arrived from London and when I heard the news about Kitty, I made haste to Longbourn."

Jane gave Aunt Philips a kiss on the cheek before turning toward the couch where Kitty and Mary sat.

"You were in London? Whatever for?" Mama queried. She returned to her seat and waited for Jane to answer, who took her time moving gracefully toward a chair closest to Kitty.

"Charles had business to attend. He has many things to take care of with all the troubles near his textile mills up North." Jane turned her attention from her mother and gazed at Kitty, her expression, as always, peaceful. "And how are you faring, Kitty? Mama's note said you were nearly killed, although you look quite fine to me."

"Oh Jane, it was dreadful. Kitty was trampled by Lord Kerr's horse." Mama's hands began to flutter toward her chest, trembling and waving about.

"Mama, Lord George's horse did not trample me." Kitty faced Jane. "He jumped over me at the last moment and I fell into the ditch."

"Still, much excitement I would presume." Jane smiled at her

Kitty could never understand how Jane kept her composure during even the most turbulent of times. She always had a kind word, regardless of how she was treated. Evidenced by how nice she remained with Charles' sister, although Caroline Bingley seemed to have undergone a drastic character transition since meeting and becoming engaged to Lord George's brother Lord Nathan.

Thoughts of Lord George caused her to smile slightly. Jane as usual noted her smile but made no comment. Instead, she focused on what happened on the road with Lord George and his horse.

"How did Lord Kerr come to almost run you over with his horse?"

"I am not sure. I had just turned off the laneway from Lucas Lodge and gone a few paces down that little incline when I heard his approach. Before I could move out of the way, he had already crested the hill and jumped over me at the very last minute."

"How frightening, and you are well? No permanent damage?" Jane cast a glance at Kitty's foot, propped up on a cushion on the couch.

71

"I have bruised ribs, which are healing and a sprained ankle. Also healing."

"Oh, my goodness, Kitty. It could have been so much more." Jane's voice wobbled.

Kitty frowned. Jane usually wasn't so perturbed.

"I am well." She hastened to comfort her sister. "Truly. Lord George brought me home safe and sound and I am none the worse for wear."

Jane's eyes glistened with tears.

"What would I do if I lost one of my sisters?"

With great practicality, Mary handed Jane a plain linen handkerchief.

"Thank you, Mary." Jane dabbed her eyes. "I do not know what has gotten into me. Lately I cry over the silliest of things. Charles is convinced he married a water pot."

"Jane, have you been feeling this way long?" Mary queried, tugging her chair closer.

"No, just these past few weeks." Jane dabbed her eyes again. "Why do you ask?"

Casting a quick peek toward their mother, still engrossed in conversation with their Aunt, Mary lowered her voice. "Have you had your monthly courses?"

"Mary!" Jane's face flushed a deep red.

"You and I have both seen Mama when she was in the first few months of carrying a baby. Think about this, Jane. You are emotional and look extremely fatigued."

"We only just arrived back from London. Of course, I am fatigued." Jane protested, twisting the handkerchief into a tight spiral, the only sign she portrayed of great emotion. Finally, she raised her gaze to Mary's. "What if I am? Please do not say anything to Mama. I will tell her when I am sure."

"Your secret is safe with us," Kitty whispered and looked at her other sister. "Is that not right, Mary?"

"To the grave." Mary replied.

Kitty settled back with a sigh. Never once had she shared a secret with Jane. Oh, she'd kept Lydia's secret and she'd keep Mary's hollowed out book quiet, but she'd never been allowed into the tight twosome of Jane and Lizzy. And then she had her very own deep, dark secret only Papa knew about and he would never tell.

"What is happening up North, Jane?" Mama called out, breaking into their conversation. "Are Charles' mills in danger of being closed down?"

"No, Mama." Jane turned in her seat to face her mother and aunt. "We are fortunate that Charles has always treated his workers fairly. Even though he introduced new machinery, he has been very careful not to cut jobs. In fact, with the expansion the machines have allowed, he has hired more men and some women as well."

"That's wonderful news. I worry so much about his business. I don't know what we'd do if he lost all his money and you had to come live with us, and then when Mr. Collins takes over Longbourn, he'll kick us all out..." Mama began to wail.

Jane rose, gave Kitty a 'forgive me' smile and went to her mother' side.

"Mama, do not worry about Charles. You forget he also has a shipping company in Liverpool. Textiles are only a small portion of his business, although lately it absorbs most of his time."

"Whatever do you mean?"

"He leaves for Lancashire tomorrow and will be gone for almost three weeks."

"You must go with him, Jane." Mama clasped Jane's hand to her bosom. "You are but newlyweds and your place is by his side."

"I have need to stay home and take care of things here." Jane extracted her hand with grace and settled on a chair near her mother.

"That will not do! You must go with him," Mama cried out. With a furtive glance toward Kitty and Mary, she hissed out, "Men have *needs*."

Once again Jane blushed deep red and both girls acted as though they'd heard nothing. Poor Jane, Kitty thought. Although Jane modulated her tone, her reply to their mother still carried over to where her younger sisters sat.

"I have no fear that Charles will stray from the marital bed, Mama. He is most faithful."

Mama blew out a harsh breath. "I still say you should keep him close. Once you are with child, then you are secure."

"I have no reason to doubt Charles, and I refuse to entertain your fears." Jane patted her mother's hand and rose to her feet. "I must return to Netherfield Park. I still have to unpack from London."

"So soon?" Mama also rose. "You didn't even have a cup of tea."

"I shall have some when I get home." Jane approached their Aunt and gave her a polite kiss on the cheek. "It was lovely to see you again, Aunt Philips. When Charles has returned from Lancashire, we shall have a dinner party."

"That would be lovely, Jane."

"Good day, Mary. I hope you heal quickly, Kitty."

Jane floated from the room and Kitty watched as their mother plopped back down in a state of agitation, looking at her sister with wide eyes.

"Oh, sister. Whatever am I going to do? Jane will lose Charles for sure." She began to weep while Aunt Philips calmly sipped her tea.

Mary caught Kitty's attention and rolled her eyes. There was no need to attend any theatres in London. They had their very own personal comedy playing out before their eyes.

DRESSED AS A COMMON laborer, George approached the servant's entrance to Creighton Castle. He'd ridden over on Mr. Bryant's horse, not wanting the servants to wonder and comment about a fine steed like Buttons. He slid off the horse, tethered him to a handy post and knocked on the heavy oak door which was opened by what he assumed was the cook.

"We're not expectin' any deliveries, what do ye want?"

George removed his cloth cap and held it to his chest, showing respect for the woman's position in the house.

"Sorry t'bother you, ma'am," he stuttered out with a York-shire drawl. "I'm 'ere t'see Mrs. Sheraton."

It had taken most of the morning, but he'd managed to coax Phillip's last name out of him. The young lad was cagey and didn't give up information easily. George knew if he gained his trust, the boy would be faithful forever and he already had plans for his future, although he wasn't about to scare Phillip away with thoughts of school and a much-needed bath.

"Mrs. Sheraton is busy with 'er duties."

The cook didn't budge, nor did she open the door further than a crack.

"I won't take much of 'er time. I know how busy a great 'ouse like this can be. I 'ave news of 'er son, Phillip."

The cook glared at him. A few long seconds passed before she nodded and said, "Stay 'ere. I'll fetch 'er."

With that she closed the door and George heard the lock sliding into place. Viscount Stanhope had trained his staff well. Breaking into his home wouldn't be easy. Not impossible, just not easy.

He waited for a few minutes and then the lock slid open again and a thin woman stood in the door frame. Although her hair was tucked beneath a mob cap, George noted that not only was the auburn shade identical to Phillip's, but also her wide blue eyes, currently filled with worry.

"You have news of my son?"

At first George was taken aback by her cultured voice. This woman had not been born into servitude. She kept checking over her shoulder, as though expecting someone to come along and interrupt them at any time.

"Aye, Mrs. Sheraton, I do."

"Is he all right? Is he alive?" Her work worn hand fluttered to her throat and her eyes filled with tears.

"No, the little blighter is fine," George hastened to assure her. "I'm 'ere to let you know 'e's workin' fer me uncle, Mr. Bryant, over at Keswick Manor. It's a 'alf mile outside the village of Northwick."

"Thank God." She swayed on her feet and leaned heavily against the open door.

"Mrs. Sheraton, are you all right?" He stepped closer, ready to catch her if she fell.

"Yes." She straightened to her full height and held his gaze. "May I visit my son when I have some time?"

"I think 'e'd like that." Seeing that determined lift to her chin reminded him of Catherine. Strong women came in many forms. "I'll take my leave." He nodded at her and placed his cap back on his head.

"Thank you for telling me in person. God bless you, Lord Kerr."

"What did you say?" George felt as though the ground had fallen from beneath his feet.

"Have no fear from me. Just take good care of my son."

Mrs. Sheraton slipped back inside the house. Once again, the locked grated across its brackets and George remained staring at the closed door. Who in the world was Mrs. Sheraton?

The next morning as George descended from the rooms above the stable, he heard a bucket hitting the floor and Phillip crying out, "Mum!" By the time he'd reached the bottom of the stairs, Mrs. Sheraton was crouched low, hugging Phillip tight in her arms. At his arrival she slowly rose.

"Mrs. Sheraton, a pleasure to see you again." George said by way of greeting.

"You know Mr. Bryant's nephew, Mum?" Phillip asked, clutching his mother's hand tight in his.

"As a matter of fact, I do. Good day to you Mr...?"

"Mr. Daniel Bryant, in case you didn't remember me first name, Mrs. Sheraton."

"Ah, yes, Daniel. I remember it now." She smiled at him and then looked down at Phillip. "What is it that you do for Mr. Bryant?"

"Ah, Mum, I look after the 'orses."

"That's horses, dearest. Remember to pronounce the 'h.'"

"No one cares if I say the 'h.'"

"I care, Phillip," Mrs. Sheraton chastised gently. "Finish your task. I have to speak with Mr. Bryant for a few moments."

"It's okay if I stay here, right Mum?" Phillip turned worried eyes toward his mother. "I won't get into any trouble."

"I know you won't. Now run along like a good boy and I shall join you shortly."

With one last glance over his shoulder, Phillip picked up the bucket and hastened down the hall to Button's stall. Once out of ear shot, George indicated with quick nod for Mrs. Sheraton to follow him out into the courtyard.

"Mrs. Sheraton..."

"We do not have much time..."

They both spoke in unison. With a slight nod, George indicated for Mrs. Sheraton to speak first.

"I haven't much time. I asked for permission to go to Northwick for some personal needs and will be expected back within the hour. Why are you here with my son, pretending to be a common laborer?"

In his line of work George often made life and death decisions based on his read of a person's character. Such was the case of Mrs. Sheraton. As she hadn't sounded the alarm at Creighton Castle when he demanded to see her, he deemed her trustworthy of his mission.

"I have reason to believe Viscount Stanhope is a traitor to England and, if possible, will break into his house and find evidence. As for your son, I met Phillip yesterday when he... well, let us say he was a young lad with time on his hands and I decided to give him honest pay for honest labor."

Neither of them broke the silence while Mrs. Sheraton, with pursed lips, absorbed what he'd said. George was about to ask if she were all right when she finally spoke.

"I can bring you in through the servant's entrance. The chimney in the front parlor has been smoking something awful. You will arrive with me to affect repairs. The Viscount isn't expected for at least a week, but there's no guarantee he won't return earlier."

George blinked at the rapidity of her statements. Never in his wildest imaginations had he ever thought to just waltz into Stanhope's house and have free rein.

"How do you know this will work?"

Mrs. Sheraton's face lit up with a beautiful smile.

"Because when Mrs. Harris, the housekeeper, heard I was going to the village, she tasked me with hiring someone to fix the chimney. I believe God almighty has provided you with a way, Lord Kerr. The question now is – will you take it?"

"Aye, Mrs. Sheraton. I'll be the best chimney sweep 'is Lordship's ever 'ad."

"Excellent," she breathed out a heavy sigh. "Next, let's discuss Phillip and his duties."

They spent the next few minutes talking about her son and George assured her he would keep Phillip safe until she could be with her children.

"Might I ask, Mrs. Sheraton, how is it that you know me?"

"My father, Mr. Power, was the vicar at Adborough Hall until his death a few years ago."

"Mr. Power was your father?"

George was completely flabbergasted. He vaguely remembered the Power's children, a boy and a girl.

"I married my husband when I was but sixteen and Phillip was born shortly thereafter. We moved here to Cambridgeshire as that's where my husband found work. He was a baker by trade. Then he enlisted and was shipped off to France. At the time, we didn't know I was pregnant with Sally." Mrs. Sheraton slipped a hanky out of a hidden pocket and dabbed at her eyes. "Poor Ronald didn't even get to set foot on French soil. He fell overboard on the crossing and drowned. With no money and nowhere to go, I took any job I could to feed my family."

"What about your brother? I remember you had a brother."

"Hamish? I do not know where he is or what he is doing. It's like he was taken from this earth on a fiery chariot. No, Lord Kerr, I was on my own with two small children and when the opportunity came to work on the Viscount's estate, I took it. My only regret is that Mrs. Puddicombe won't let me see my babies as much as I'd like."

George hesitated about telling her Phillip no longer stayed at Mrs. Puddicombe's. He decided to leave it alone. For now, Phillip was safe with him and they'd deal with Mrs. Sheraton's daughter at a later date.

Phillip returned and hugged his mother tight around the waist.

"I'm so glad you're 'ere... here, Mum."

"I love you so much Phillip and want you to stay with Lor—, Mr. Bryant, and I will come see you in a few days."

"All right," Phillip sniffled into her skirts. Mrs. Sheraton crouched down, placed both hands on top of his thin shoulders and made him look her in the eye.

"Phillip, listen to me carefully. I trust Mr. Bryant more than you could ever imagine and know he will keep you safe. Will you promise to stay here so I won't worry about you?"

Several seconds crawled by before Phillip nodded his head. Mrs. Sheraton pulled him close and hugged him. "That's my darling boy." She then stood and faced George.

"If you have any tools, Mr. Bryant, bring them along. You may as well return to the house with me so you can fix the chimney." She turned to her son and leaned down to give him a kiss on the cheek. "Watch the stars, Phillip and know that I am looking at them with you and remember to say your prayers."

"Yes, Mum." Phillip looked at George with eyes full of tears. "Is there anything you need me to do, Mr. Bryant?"

Against his will, George felt the strings of his heart tug. Where was that cold detachment he was so proud of?

"Make sure Buttons has a good brushing and clean out the rest of the stalls before laying new hay. I've heard the owner is bringing his horses here over the next few weeks."

A spark of interest flickered in Phillip's eyes, chasing away the sadness for a few brief seconds.

"Yes, sir," he said and with a little wave at his mother, turned back toward the stable.

George gathered some tools and joined Mrs. Sheraton on the county road. As they walked toward Stanhope's estate, Mrs. Sheraton filled him in on who worked within the big house.

"I will introduce you to Mrs. Harris. When you are shown into the parlor she'll assign a footman to you. If she trusts you, she'll assign John. He's the short one and quite lazy. He'll stay out in the corridor and won't care what you do. If she deems you untrustworthy, she'll assign Thomas. He'll come into the room with you and report everything to Mrs. Harris who in turn will report it to Stanhope."

"Got it. Be on my best behavior for Mrs. Harris and Thomas. Anything else?"

"One of my duties is to bank the ashes in the fireplaces every evening. For the next three nights, I will make sure the window to the Viscount's study is not latched. His study is the room adjacent to the parlor you will be working in. I don't know if you can gain entry during the day while you're there, that's up to you to figure out."

George marveled at the way Mrs. Sheraton's mind worked. The War Office could use a few people of her caliber and wondered if he could somehow introduce her to Evangeline. Together they would make a formidable team. Napoleon wouldn't stand a chance against the likes of them.

By this time, they'd arrived at the estate. He tugged his hat low over his eyes and walked with a swaying gait, as though he were heavier in weight than he truly was. Within minutes, he'd been introduced to Mrs. Harris, who in turn sent him off to the parlor with Thomas.

Chapter Six

"Have a care, Kitty. We do not want you falling and re-injuring your ribs."

Mrs. Bennet cautioned Kitty as she stepped outside for the first time since the accident, placing her weight on a walking stick Papa had given her. Originally grandfather's, Papa relayed the story of how Great-Grandfather Bennet used the stick on his grand tour of Europe, hiking through the mountains of Switzerland. She had no intent of traversing a mountain, or even Mount Oakham. The little garden outside would suffice.

"I will walk with you, Kitty."

Mary exited the house and began to keep pace with her, which was about the rate of a snail.

"Thank you, Mary," she said between clenched teeth. "My goal is to make it to the small bench beneath the oak tree, stay there for five days and then return to the house."

Mary laughed gaily. "You walk almost as much as Lizzy. I think you will be up and about in no time. Careful here."

Mary moved aside and allowed Kitty to skirt a puddle in the path. The rain had finally let up, for which she was grateful. Nobody wanted to return to the house with their hems six inches deep in mud. She grinned at the memory of Lizzy's story about Miss Bingley's reaction to her appearance after walking the three miles to Netherfield Park when Jane took ill.

"Well, you made it," Mary commented when they reached the bench. "What would you like to do now?"

"I think I shall rest for a moment and then continue."

Kitty settled on the bench and used the walking stick to raise her foot off the ground. Yesterday, Papa showed her how to prop the cane against a piece of furniture, such as the garden bench and then place her foot on the stick. He'd told her, with a derisive laugh, how he'd injured his own ankle playing cricket at Cambridge.

She loved the attention he bestowed upon her, knowing how much he missed his Lizzy and her quick mind. Kitty never tried to compete with her sister for Papa's attention. How could she? Most of her time she'd chased after Lydia, trying to no avail to keep her out of trouble. Much good that did her. Lydia still behaved with the utmost impropriety and, as always, someone else cleaned up her mess. Thank goodness for Mr. Darcy.

For almost a quarter hour Papa had regaled Kitty with stories of his time spent at Cambridge, until a shadow crossed his face. She knew, without him saying a word, his thoughts had traveled to one classmate in particular and the pleasantness of the moment slipped away. With a 'you're a good girl, Kitty' and a pat on her hand, Papa retreated to his book room and when he attended supper that night, his eyes were red-rimmed and bloodshot.

The guilt she wore like a heavy shawl sometimes threatened to overwhelm her. With a small sniff, to keep the tears at bay, she shook her head and struggled to stand, waving off Mary's helping hand. The past was the past. What was done could not be undone and she'd have all her empty life to reflect on it.

"Let us keep going, Mary." She leaned on the stick and began walking around the edge of the garden. "I am determined to surprise Mr. Wilson when he arrives on the morrow."

"I think you should head back to the house. What if you overtax your ankle and re-injure it?"

Kitty took another few steps and conceded Mary was right.

"All right." She turned and started toward the house. "Last one there gets to choose the game for tonight."

"You are pretty cheeky for a turtle," Mary laughed out. "I am tempted to dawdle, if only to win."

"You know I would like to play Dictionary. It is the only way to keep Mama from hovering. Do you think we could invite Papa to join us?"

"Good gracious, no! If we best him at Dictionary his world would turn upside down."

"True, but maybe we were wrong, allowing him to think we are silly girls."

They both walked in silence, broken only by Kitty's puffs of air as she struggled with the walking stick. Finally, they reached the parlor doors and she collapsed on the closest chair.

"We should invite Papa," Mary said after Kitty had regained her breath.

"What changed your mind?"

A sly grin lifted the corners of Mary's lips.

"We shall wager extra pin money for our trip to London. Papa will never suspect we could win."

"You are devious, Mary. But Papa is very learned and well-read, he may win. What can we wager in return?"

"Complete silence and no interruptions for one month upon our return."

Mary's eyes sparkled and Kitty chuckled before saying, "We should invite Papa."

They nodded in agreement.

After dinner, they cajoled their father into a game of Dictionary and before a half hour passed, Mr. Bennet was down two pounds. Surprised, and secretly pleased, he didn't mind having his purse lessened and spent the rest of his evening wondering how he'd missed the fact that his two remaining daughters had such an extensive grasp of the English language.

He determined to peruse his dictionary on the morrow, and if they challenged him again, he'd be ready. Silence for one month complete was too precious to lose.

THE FIRST DAY IN STANHOPE'S parlor, George concentrated strictly on the chimney itself and quickly determined it required a new damper. Thomas watched him like the proverbial hawk, straying no more than three feet away at any given time. George received perverse pleasure in accidentally bumping into him as he moved around, making sure to transfer soot from his clothing onto Thomas's pristine footman's tunic. Later, in the afternoon, his ploy was rewarded as Thomas kept careful watch near the door but came no further into the room.

"Mrs. Harris wants you to clean the master's fireplace in the study," Thomas said when he arrived the second day.

"Aye. I'll take a look after I've checked out the roof." He lumbered by Thomas and proceeded outside.

He had permission to enter the study, but with Thomas hovering like a mother hen, there wouldn't be much chance to scope out the room. He'd have to wait until that evening. As it was, when he'd descended from the roof, after checking out the mantle and flashings, the footman John stood outside the study door.

"Where's the other bloke?" George asked John.

"Mrs. Harris has another assignment for him." John replied, his tone indicating the assignment had nothing to do with work. "How come you don't got a climbing boy?"

George knew most chimney sweeps employed small children to climb inside the chimney to remove the soot.

"Don't need no climbers today. I'll bring the little blighter tomorrow, if 'e hasn't run off." George walked past the footman into the parlor, then turned and gave him a curious look when he didn't trail behind like Thomas had. John didn't know he had the inside scoop from Mrs. Sheraton. "Ain't you gonna watch me? I might decide to pilfer a few pretty baubles."

"I wouldn't if were you. 'is Lordship's right mean if crossed." John's attention was diverted by a maid walking down the hall. "Besides, I got better things to do. Why, hello, Betsy..."

George entered the study and partially closed the door. He could still hear the banter and innuendo, coupled with a few giggles, but the two servants paid him no attention. All he needed was a few precious minutes to rifle through Stanhope's desk. He laid a blanket in front of the fireplace, removed the thick gloves he'd worn and moved back to the desk. Wasting no time, he opened one drawer after another, discovering nothing of import or anything out of place. The only thing of interest was a small miniature of a young girl, secured by a ribbon to a packet of letters. She looked vaguely familiar, however if she were Stanhope's daughter, it would stand to reason she'd have some of his features. Poor girl.

He quickly checked the address on the letters, to determine if this was where the French connection could be found, but they were addressed to a law firm in London. He recognized the name and notched another strike against Stanhope. The man who owned the firm was notoriously corrupt and ruthless. George filed the name away in his mind. When he had time, he'd pull it back out and digest this morsel of news.

He pushed away from the desk and with a practiced eye studied the room. If he wanted to hide something, where would the most likely place be? His gaze drifted across a large bookcase, a richly embroidered Queen Anne chair with a small table and lamp beside it, past the fireplace he was supposed to be working on and finally a cumbersome, heavily tufted divan. He moved over to the bookcase and studied the titles. George was almost through the second row when the pitch of voices changed outside the door.

Quickly, he moved to the chimney and pulled on his work gloves. He'd just reached up the chimney with one arm when the door opened fully. Mrs. Harris stood in the entrance, a deep scowl on her face. Almost as though she were angry at finding him working.

He lowered his arm and shook off the soot onto the blanket, stood and faced her.

"Can I do anything fer ye, Mrs. 'arris?"

"You've been here two days. What is wrong with the chimney in the parlor?"

"The mantle, flashings and cricket work just fine." George quietly thanked God for his useful memory of trivial facts. He scratched his head through the dirty, woolen cap. "I removed the damper. It's cracked which made it difficult to move and blocked the flue."

"Can it be fixed?" she demanded.

"Aye. Got one back at me shop and can replace it on the morrow."

"Good. The Viscount may return at any moment and I want this mess cleaned up."

"Aye, Mrs. 'arris. This chimney only needs a good cleaning, nothing more. I'll be gone afore 'e's back."

She gave him a curt nod and left the room, the keys attached to her chatelaine clanging with every angry step. Oh yes. He'd be long gone by the time Stanhope returned, hopefully with evidence of his treacherous allegiance to France. Tonight, he'd return through the study window Mrs. Sheraton had promised to leave unsecured.

THAT NIGHT, NEARING midnight, he crept through the ornamental bushes beneath the study window. With the moon at near fullness and the sky clear of clouds, he had no trouble moving around in the dark. The only thing that could alert the night patrol was Stanhope's dog. However, George had befriended the beast, bringing him treats over the past two days and allowed the animal to learn his scent. If the dog did show up, he'd be rewarded with a nice scrap of cooked ham and not raise the alarm.

Without much fuss, he gained entry to the study, pulled the heavy curtains across the window, lit the candle he'd brought and began a thorough search of the room. No book was out of place, nothing was hidden under any cushions or even beneath the area rug. Frustrated, he sat behind the desk.

If he were Stanhope, where would he hide important papers? He placed the candle holder on the desk and leaned back deep in thought, his index finger worrying his lower lip. His contemplative gaze fell on the opposite wall and it was then he noticed that the flickering of the candle light revealed a slight incongruity with the painting hung over the fireplace. It seemed as though the shadows were deeper on one side.

Feeling a familiar thrum of excitement, he moved toward the picture and studied its frame. The left edge of the painting was a quarter of an inch further from the wall than the right edge. Following a hunch, he grasped the right edge of the painting and pulled. Quietly, the painting swung open like a small door and revealed a hollowed-out niche filled with packages and documents.

The grandfather clock in the main hall chimed the hour three times and soon the junior servants would be starting their daily chores. He grabbed whatever documents were in the cubby hole and stuffed them into the satchel he'd brought. After returning the portrait to its original position he snuffed out the candle and slipped through the study window into the bushes.

Streaks of faint light had painted the sky with subdued hues of orange and yellow by the time he entered his room at the stable. He'd snag a few hours of sleep before returning to Creighton Castle to fix the fireplace. Later, after sorting through the papers, he'd return whatever was not incriminating. No need to alert Stanhope of his theft right away. The longer the Viscount thought his documents were safe, the more time George had to further set the trap.

He congratulated himself on how easy this mission had been, almost too easy. It was only when his head hit the pillow and he had begun to drift into the hazy world of Morpheus did he remember he'd left the candle lamp on the fireplace mantle.

Chapter Seven

D awn was but a few hours old when George finally quit the bed and opened the satchel. He quickly determined most documents were of no interest to him, with exception of a copy of Stanhope's last will and testament, dated some twelve years prior. All properties and titular deeds went to the closest living heir, which was a daughter, Harriet. He thought back to the miniature of the young girl found with the bundle of letters addressed to the law firm in London. She must be his daughter and as George had never heard reference to any living child, he wondered why Stanhope hadn't revised his will.

About to close the ledger he noticed the edges of the spine were not lined up. He turned it back over in his hand and a quick perusal showed the inside flap had indeed been tampered with. Carefully, he picked at the corner and whatever glue used to reseal the page pulled away with ease. Inside, a thin vellum paper lay folded. His heart rate quickened at the evidence before him. Viscount Stanhope was not only a Lord for the realm of England, he was a distant cousin of Phillippe de Segur, one of Napoleon's closest friends and aide de camp. Such troubling connections to Napoleon made Stanhope a dangerous man indeed. There was also another folded note.

Scribbled across the top was, *L'Angleterre comme une République Libre*. What was Stanhope involved with that wanted England as a Free Republic? There followed a list of names. Not necessarily full nomenclatures, but acronyms, such as: Lord M, Sir R, etc., etc. In total five persons were indicated and underneath them were the initials P.W. - which had been crossed out - and S.P. written beside the blotted-out initials.

He felt a chill shiver down his spine as he studied the initials P.W. followed by S.P. and a sense of dread filled his heart. If this was what he thought, there was a greater conspiracy at large and if successful, would change the landscape of England forever. It was vital he brought these documents to Lord Grayson as soon as possible. He placed these two documents into his traveling bag. The ledger and rest of the papers he slid back into the satchel and after washing his face in cold water, dressed for his last day as a common laborer.

"GOOD DAY, MRS. 'ARRIS."

George arrived at Creighton Castle a few minutes after eight a.m. Greeted by the irate housekeeper, he removed his hat and gave her a polite nod.

"You are expected to be about your duties by precisely seven a.m. Your wages will reflect this tardiness."

He clutched the hat a little tighter. If he were a working man, losing any amount of wage could be devastating. In keeping with his role, he bowed his head again.

"Me chimney climber died last night. I 'ad to pay respect to 'is family," he lied with a smoothness born from years of practice in the art of subterfuge.

"Your hired help is of no concern to me, Mr. Bryant. Wages will be deducted. Now please attend your duties and advise John when you are finished."

"Aye, Mrs. 'arris," George mumbled, keeping his eyes on the floor.

Her skirts flared slightly as she turned in a huff and once again her chatelaine and keys jangled with every step. A grin threatened to mar his image of humility. The fact she wore those keys like a prize worked to his advantage. It was patently obvious she wore them with pride, showcasing her position of authority. He likened them to tying a bell on a cat to warn the birds. Mrs. Harris announced her impending arrival to all the household staff who made sure they were diligent in their duties. That is, until she walked away.

He shuffled to the parlor and John met him at the door to the study.

"I'll finish with the damper and be on my way." He noticed John glaring into the room, a scowl on his face. "What's bit your arse this morning?"

"Mrs. Sheraton's in there. I don't like the way she looks at me."

"And 'ow is that?" George asked, his eyebrow raised slightly at John's comment.

"Like she's better 'n the rest of us. All that fancy schoolin' don't count for nothin' here."

George shrugged, not wishing to get into a discussion with the footman.

"Well, I never met the woman, so I don't got no problems wif 'her."

He moved past John into the study and without looking at Mrs. Sheraton, who was busy dusting the bookshelves, approached the fireplace. The candle was not where he left it. He placed his bag by his feet and laid the drop cloth in front of the fireplace. Mrs. Sheraton continued dusting, moving closer to the fireplace with each swipe.

"You are late. Mrs. Harris has been in high dudgeon all morning," she whispered.

Assured that John had moved from the door, he risked a glance at Mrs. Sheraton.

"Why is that?"

"The Viscount returns late this afternoon. She wants this room spic and span."

"Watch the door for me. I have no time to waste."

He heard a small gasp from Mrs. Sheraton when he pulled the documents out of the bag, swung the portrait open and placed them inside. Satisfied they were arranged in the same order as he'd found them, he closed the portrait and began rolling up the drop cloth.

"I left a candle on the mantlepiece. Have you seen it, or did Mrs. Harris discover it first?"

"Pray do not worry, Lord Kerr. I told Mrs. Harris the candle was mine. That I must have forgotten it last night after cleaning around the fireplace."

"Thank you. Did she believe you? The last thing I wish to do is place you in danger."

"No need to thank me. I've given Mrs. Harris no cause to doubt my word, so far. As for being in danger... I know the Viscount's a vile man and have no way to prove it. If it weren't for the children I would have long left his employ."

Sadly, George understood exactly why she stayed. There weren't many jobs that a genteel woman could perform and maintain her dignity. He'd seen the seedy side of life too much to pretend otherwise.

"I have some things to clean up outside prior to leaving."

"I wouldn't waste time, Lord Kerr. The longer you stay, the more dangerous it becomes."

"There may be footprints below the study window."

"Taken care of."

"You astound me, Mrs. Sheraton."

She laughed softly. "I had a younger brother who was forever slipping out of the house, escaping the 'dour Mr. Power', as you and your brothers liked to call him."

George gave a start at the familiar nickname he and his brothers had bestowed upon their father's vicar.

"We meant no disrespect—"

"And none was taken," she hastened to reassure him. "My father was difficult to live with at times, which was why Hamish longed to find his freedom. Because of that, I quickly learned the most efficient way to smooth out muddy footprints and remove debris from window sills."

"Once again, I cannot thank you enough."

"Quite the opposite. I should be thanking you. The fact you are providing refuge for my son has me forever in your debt."

When Stanhope realized his documents had been stolen, literally out from under his nose, he'd leave no stone unturned in finding out who aided the thief. It would take little digging to learn Mrs. Sheraton was the one who brought George into the house in the guise of a chimney sweep.

"Mrs. Sheraton, I have a proposition..."

HE FEARED FOR HER SAFETY and before quitting Creighton Castle asked her to quietly pack up her stuff and flee to his estate. While waiting for her to arrive at Keswick Manor, he changed into his traveling clothes and made his way to the main house. There he spoke with the aging housekeeper, Mrs. Walbush about his plans to re-open the manor.

"I'm so glad you stopped in, Lord George. It does my heart good to know this lovely house will be of use again and to see you as well."

"Thank you, Mrs. Walbush. I have been neglectful, but it is high time I take up the reins and learn how to run an estate."

"God bless you, Lord George."

"If you require anything, advise Mr. Piper. As Mother's steward he has the address of our solicitors and they can forward any funds required."

"When do you want things at the ready, sir?"

"After Lady Addlesworth's Midsummer's Ball. I shall arrive shortly thereafter."

Mrs. Walbush clasped her hands together. George noted her uncomfortable fidgeting.

"Is there something you wish to discuss, Mrs. Walbush?"

"Yes. I was about to write the Duchess about my decision, but seeing as you are here, I'll give my notice to you then."

"Your notice!"

"I'm not getting any younger, Lord George." She treated him to rare smile. "I've been housekeeper of Keswick Manor nigh unto thirty years and was housemaid a good fifteen prior to that. These bones are weary and I'm afraid I won't be able to keep up with the demands of a full house."

"You have been a loyal servant, Mrs. Walbush. Much of my childhood memories hinge around your dedication and care." His mind turned over at a rapid pace at her announcement. "Have you anyone in mind as your replacement?"

"Oh no, sir. I'd only made the decision a few weeks ago."

"Then I have a suggestion. There will be a Mrs. Sheraton arriving sometime today. She has been in the employ of Viscount Stanhope. Circumstances have arisen which have forced her to leave his establishment."

At Mrs. Walbushs' pursed lips, he hastened to assure her.

"There was nothing untoward with her character. She aided me in a risky endeavor and I fear for her safety. I offered her shelter and work here. Her son, Phillip is already working with Mr. Bryant in the stables."

"Oh yes, Phillip. Such a sweet boy."

"He is, and his mother is a good woman. I propose you take her under your wing and show her how Keswick Manor is run. When you retire, she can move into the role of housekeeper with ease."

"Is there anything else I should know about Mrs. Sheraton, M'Lord?"

For a brief moment, George hesitated, but Mrs. Walbush had been a loyal employee for over forty-five years. If he couldn't trust her, then he couldn't trust anyone.

"Her father was our vicar at Adborough Hall. If anyone – and I mean *anyone* other than me or my family – ask about Mrs. Sheraton, you are to say you have never seen her. That you do not know her and advise me directly at Kerr House in London. Her very life depends on your discretion."

Mrs. Walbushs' eyebrows rose higher and higher with each word until they threatened to disappear completely under her mob cap. Just as quickly, her face smoothed and she stood a little straighter, shoulders back, chin jutted out with determination.

"She will be safe here, Lord George. Might I make a suggestion we call her something besides Mrs. Sheraton. Perhaps something like Mrs. Nelson. This way, the maids or other staff won't inadvertently 'spill the beans', so to speak."

"That is a wonderful suggestion."

"I'll also tell them Mrs. Nelson is my great-niece from..."

"Yorkshire, as that is where Adborough Hall is located."

"From Yorkshire then, and she worked for the former Duke as well as your brother, the current Duke. That should satisfy any curiosity about her sudden arrival."

"This should not prove too difficult, Mrs. Walbush, as Mrs. Sheraton has much knowledge of the area and can pull this off with ease. You will find her a quick study."

They spent a few more minutes discussing the housekeeper's suite and how they could situate both children, if needed.

"Phillip may choose to stay with Mr. Bryant, near the stables, but her daughter is still too young to be left alone."

"If she doesn't take the housekeeper's suite, there are some lovely cottages on the property and there's always a young mother willing to look after another child to bring in extra money." Mrs. Walbush suggested.

"Excellent. I will leave this in your capable hands."

"Are you dining here tonight, sir?"

"Yes, I will partake in a light supper and break my fast at dawn. I want to get an early start back to London."

"Very good, My Lord. I'll advise Cook."

Satisfied Mrs. Sheraton was safe, George took to his bedroom for much needed rest. it wouldn't do to fall asleep upon Buttons. Early tomorrow morning he'd leave for Hertfordshire and Miss Catherine Bennet. In the midst of all the intrigue he'd found his thoughts straying to her at the oddest times and was anxious to see her again. To discover whether his distraction was but a passing fancy, or something more tangible.

"WHAT DO YOU THINK, Mary? Should I wear the light-yellow bonnet, or the pink one?"

Mary paused in the hall and came to the door of Kitty's room. With mild horror, she surveyed the pile of clothes on her sister's bed, threatening to topple over.

"You have not begun to pack?"

Kitty threw her hands in the air and flopped into the chair beside her bed.

"No. I cannot make up my mind of what to wear tomorrow. I do not have anything appropriate. All my dresses, with the exception of the lovely gown I wore at Lizzy's wedding, are sprigged muslin. We will look like country misses."

"That is because we *are* country misses." Mary said in a soothing voice. "I believe you could wear a sack cloth dress and Lord Kerr would still be enamored. He did not even flinch when you were covered in mud and weeds."

"I am not worried about what Lord George thinks," Kitty lied, looking down at her hands. If she told herself enough times to forget the way he made her feel, it would happen. "I have never been to London and do not want to be embarrassed."

"Mmm hmm," Mary hummed. "I am not fooled by you any more, Catherine Bennet. You are in a dither over Lord Kerr and I do not know why you will not admit that. If he pursues you, will you accept a courtship from him?"

"No!" Horrified, Kitty's wide-eyed gaze flew up to her sister's. "I could never accept a courtship from him."

"Why ever not?" Slack jawed, Mary could only stare.

Too late, she realized she'd said more than intended. Tears pooled in her eyes and she willed them to not fall.

"I am unworthy of his regard, and that is all I can say."

Mary came and kneeled beside the chair, taking her cold hands in her warm ones.

"Kitty, you are not unworthy. You are a child of God and He is the only one that counts. You are worthy in His eyes." She stood and released Kitty's hands. "Pray about this sister. I do not know what your burden is, but I see it is a heavy one. If you cannot share them with me, then cast your cares upon Him and He will lighten your load."

"Thank you, Mary. I already have. I also have a bad habit of picking that load back up after I finish praying."

"Silly girl. Well, I will add my prayers to yours and see if one of these days that dirty bag stays at the foot of the cross." Mary moved toward the door and with a backward glance toward the pile of clothes, said, "Wear the yellow muslin and brown spencer. With your coloring, that dress looks most becoming. Pair it up with the matching bonnet and trim."

The next hour was spent packing her trunk and setting aside some things that needed mending. Her mood vacillated between excitement and dread, not abating until she descended to join Mama and Mary in the parlor. She'd reached the bottom stair when Papa came to the door of his book room. That he'd been waiting for her was evident.

"Before you leave for Town, I must have a word with you."

She followed her father into his book room and waited as he paced to his desk. Papa was in an unfamiliar state of agitation.

"We have never spoken of that terrible time and you need to know you were NOT responsible." She knew exactly of what time he spoke of. "The fault lies with me. Do not let this stop you from accepting the affections of a decent man."

Her chest constricted and although she wanted to flee from the room, her feet were rooted to the floor while tears coursed down her cheeks. Papa came to where she stood, frozen, and drew her close. With a gentle hand he guided her head against his chest and simply held her as great sobs wracked her body. They stood in this attitude for several minutes before he began to pat her on the back.

"There, there, child. Dry your face and fix your hair. The Lucas' and Longs will be here shortly and your mother has gone to great trouble for your final meal before you leave."

"Yes, Papa." Kitty swiped a hand across her cheeks, thankfully accepting the fine linen handkerchief her father handed to her. "I will do my best."

"I know you will."

She prepared to leave and moved slowly toward the door.

"Kitty?"

At his calling she turned to face him.

"Yes, Papa," she whispered.

"I may not say this to you often – if ever, come to think of it – but I am exceedingly proud of you. Never forget I love you very much and wish I had never taken you with me."

"It is not your fault, Papa. How could we have known?"

"As your father, I should have taken more care."

"I do not blame you in any way."

"No, Kitty. As I once said to Lizzy with regard to Lydia, I need to feel how much I am to blame. I am not afraid of being overpowered by the impression as I am sure it will soon pass but allow me to regret not keeping a closer eye on my daughter."

Instead of exiting, she impulsively ran to him and before he could move, kissed him briefly on the cheek and almost flew out of the room. Had she looked back, she would have seen a stunned look on her father's face as he lifted trembling fingers to his cheek. She then ran upstairs to clean the remaining vestiges of her tears away. For the first time since that horrid night she realized Papa carried as much guilt as her, and also for the first time, in some strange way, no longer felt alone.

DINNER WAS A LONG DRAWN out affair. Both Sir William Lucas and Kitty's best friend Maria teased her mercilessly about Lord George. Her heartfelt hope that his brief visit wouldn't create a stir among the families of Meryton had been wishful thinking.

"I suppose dinners at Lord Kerr's estate will be much grander than this, Mrs. Bennet. Not that you'd mind if it means your daughter's future is secure," Sir William bellowed from his seat. That he was pleased with what he thought was a witty remark was evidenced by jiggling jowls, bright merry eyes and the utterance of 'Capital' many times.

Kitty clenched her fists beneath the table, grateful for Mary's hand briefly touching her elbow, giving silent support. Across the table she noticed Jane purse her lips in displeasure and she even dared to glare down the table at Sir William. For a brief moment Kitty almost let out a chuckle. Her normally placid sister displayed unusual emotions, something she'd heard whispered about by women who'd borne children. How husbands tended to tread carefully, not knowing which way their wife's emotions could swing from one hour to the next. It seemed Jane was experiencing this same phenomenon.

Dinner finally concluded and the ladies repaired to the sitting room. They hadn't been separated for more than five minutes when Mrs. Long, seated next to Mama and Lady Lucas, mused out loud, "No need to play dancing music tonight Mary. Your sister's partner won't arrive at Longbourn until the morrow."

Kitty's cheeks burned with embarrassment, angry Mama did not correct their ill-advised opinions. Mary, seated on the couch opposite, looked at her with quiet pity. Mrs. Long continued with her mean-spirited gossip, adding one sly innuendo on top of another. Mama did nothing to stem the tide until Jane finally stood and faced the three women in the corner.

"Mrs. Long, please stop speculating on Lord George Kerr. He has neither given nor received undue attention to or from Kitty. Other than returning her to Longbourn safe and sound in an unorthodox manner, I have been told he was a perfect gentleman after their unfortunate encounter." Jane's voice was quiet, as always, but anyone with an ear to hear knew there was tempered steel beneath the velvet tones. Her eldest sister had laid down the gauntlet of proper behavior and now dared their mother's friend to pick it up.

Never before had one of her siblings defended her so vigorously, not even Lydia, and they'd been so close at one time. Kitty's heart swelled with such love for her eldest sister. Jane would not stand meekly by while Mama embarrassed her in such a public venue. Not after her near miss with Charles because of her antics.

"Well said, Jane." Their father spoke up from the far side of the room where he and the other gentleman had entered. "I spoke at length with Lord George and his intentions are quite honorable, which is refreshing from someone with noble birth."

Kitty's cheeks burned at her father's oblique reference to what they'd spoken about earlier. How grateful she was that no one else knew why he was so embittered. Everyone would think she blushed because of reference to Lord George. It didn't help that her own mother delighted in fanning the flames of raging gossip. Maybe now with Papa endorsing Lord George's character, she and Mary could safely travel to London without fear of a marriage announcement appearing in the newspaper.

"Oh, Mr. Bennet," cried Mama. "You know I want nothing but the best for our dear Kitty and mark my words, that young man likes her. Very much, I believe."

"Believe what you will, Mrs. Bennet, the banns shall not be read before our daughters leave for London." Mr. Bennet looked around the room. "Now, let us play some cards. With her bad leg, this is an activity my beautiful daughter *can* partake of."

With that announcement, all teasing stopped and soon everybody was involved in several games of whist. Once the shock of hearing her father call her beautiful wore off, Kitty enjoyed the rest of the evening, winning several rounds with Papa as her partner.

Chapter Eight

Kitty awoke at the crack of dawn. Sunlight streamed through the window and prisms of color, reflected off the dressing table mirror, danced across the wall. She rolled onto her side and lay for a full three minutes savoring this moment of quiet, broken only by the cocky little birds who deigned to greet the new day with song.

Her trunk lay open at the end of her bed awaiting her daily toiletries and other sundry items. There was nothing more for her to do other than dress, break her fast and wait for Lord George's arrival. An express had arrived just as their guests were starting to leave, informing them he'd arrive at Longbourn no later than eleven a.m. Five hours until he arrived. With a soft groan, she rolled onto her back and stared at the ceiling. Already the wait was interminable and only five minutes had passed. How would she survive another five hours and more?

Knowing their maid would attend her room to stoke the fires, Kitty sat up and swung her legs over the edge of the bed. Her ankle and calf still sported a shockingly purple bruise, tinged with hints of green and orange. She was grateful the swelling was all but gone and she could finally put some weight upon her foot. The side of her body also looked like a map she'd once seen in a book Papa kept in his book room. It was of the continent of Africa, with each known country displayed in a different color.

With slow steps she made her way to the water closet and began her morning ablutions. By the time Sarah entered and began poking the coals in her fireplace she was dressed and had begun to braid her hair for the day.

"Oh, Miss Kitty, you've got such lovely hair, 'tis a shame to hide it beneath a bonnet."

"Thank you, Sarah, but I am traveling to London and do not want to appear like I am a slow-witted country miss who does not know the proper etiquette of a young lady. No respectable woman would be seen with her hair down in public." Kitty smiled at Sarah through the mirror. "What is allowed at Longbourn will not be borne by the elite of London."

"I still say 'tis a shame to hide all them glorious curls, but you're right about what's allowed with family." Sarah finished stoking the fire and hurried behind Kitty. "Allow me to fix your hair, then you can break your fast. Cook prepared all your and Mary's favorites."

Kitty murmured a 'thank you' and left Sarah to pin up her hair, who happily hummed a popular song while she worked. She'd miss the rhythm of Longbourn. Even when the house was full of girls and the halls practically vibrated from shouts and giggles, and squabbles over ribbons and buttons, there was a certain comfort in what was familiar.

Mary met her at the head of the stairs and walked patiently behind her as they descended to the main floor. The scent of fresh baked bread and cooked ham greeted them when they entered the breakfast room and her stomach rumbled.

"You look lovely, Kitty. Have you done something different with your hair?" Mama asked as she and Mary made for their seats.

"Yes, thank you, Mama."

"And you look as well as you can, Mary."

"Thank you, Mama."

Kitty lowered her eyes in attempt to hide a sudden burst of anger. Why must Mama always belittle Mary? Next to Jane, Mary was the only daughter who never gave their parents cause to worry. Did she moralize a little too much at times? Most assuredly, but given her new found knowledge of her sister's psyche, Kitty knew Mary's heart was in the right place and didn't mind when her sister shared a bit of God's word while they'd exercised her ankle these past few days.

Conversely, the more Kitty accepted Mary as she was, the less she proselytized. Indeed, Kitty was convinced the moral platitudes her elder sister dropped in the middle of conversations over the past year was her way of dealing with Lydia's behavior. Maybe Mama didn't like to be reminded how she'd failed in curbing Lydia's exuberance.

"Here are my erudite daughters," Papa exclaimed as he entered the breakfast room.

"Erudite, Mr. Bennet?" Mama's brow furrowed. "Whatever do you mean?"

"I am delighted to report that we have the brightest jewels in all of Hertfordshire within these walls, Mrs. Bennet. Not only did my daughters defeat me in Dictionary, they also managed to lighten my pocket."

"Lighten your pocket? Whatever are you talking about."

Kitty raised her gaze to her father's and silently implored him not to reveal she and Mary each had a one pound note in their reticules. If Mama knew, the money would be sent off to Lydia before they'd even entered the carriage for London.

"I gave them each a treat, my dear. A well earned treat, one they will not receive on our next challenge."

Mary smiled wide at Kitty. They'd known their father would not let the challenge lapse.

"We will not be back for a few months, Papa. You shall have plenty of time to study." Mary teased as she dropped a dollop of preserve on her heavily buttered scone.

"Gloat now daughter, for you will not get the chance next time we test our knowledge. You and your sister surprised me the other evening, but now the advantage is mine."

"Mr. Bennet. Whatever are you talking about?"

"Mary and I challenged Papa to a game of Dictionary last night, Mama."

Mama's mouth fell slightly open, as though she were about to say something and had forgotten what it was. She also had a perplexed air about her. Kitty couldn't help but smirk. For years their father proclaimed they were the silliest girls in all of England, and by tacit understanding, their mother agreed. Now, Papa praised and teased them the same way he and Lizzy treated each other. Truly, Mama's world must be tilting just a little.

"You and Mary challenged Mr. Bennet?" Mrs. Bennet turned slightly dazed eyes toward Kitty. "And won?"

"Yes, Mama."

"Were you ill, Mr. Bennet?"

"No, my dear," he said with a laugh. "I most certainly was not ill, but I was definitely caught in a sneak attack."

After that interchange, conversation turned to the weather and how long their trip to London would take.

"Make sure my brother takes you to the best warehouses. Your Aunt Gardiner has an eye for fashion, although I think she uses too little lace, and I won't be there to supervise. I think you should each have a new pair of boots. You're both still growing and I'm sure you could use a new pair of dancing slippers—"

"Enough Mrs. Bennet. You shall spend all their dowry money before they have a beau."

"Mr. Bennet! They have never been to London like Jane and Lizzy, and you never denied them a dress or two."

"Quite right. How thoughtless of me. One dress each along with a pair of sturdy boots, but no dancing slippers. I do not think your brother and his wife shall be escorting our daughters to many balls."

"You forget they will also be staying with Lizzy and Mr. Darcy and meeting other rich families who may have single sons in want of a wife." Mama threw her linen napkin onto her plate and rose to her feet in agitation. "Would you deny your daughters the chance to make a good impression?"

"I forget nothing, Madam." Papa also stood. "If you want them to have the fripperies a fortune can purchase, then I give you permission to ask your daughter's rich husbands to provide them with what I cannot."

With that, Papa strode out of the breakfast room and Mama gaped after him.

"What did I say?" she asked no one in particular and flopped back into her chair.

Kitty waited for almost a half hour before she dared knock on the door to Papa's book room.

"Enter."

She pushed open the door and found him in his favorite chair, book in hand, a cup of tea on the side table. He closed the book after inserting a piece of paper to keep his place and then gave her his full attention.

"You have come to chastise me for my outburst."

He didn't pose it as a question, but as a statement. She came further in the room and sat on the tufted footstool by his chair.

"Mary and I do not require any new clothing. What we have is sufficient."

"My child. I would give you all sorts of fripperies if that were possible, but your papa has not managed his money as well as he should. However, your clever brother Mr. Darcy has been writing me most diligently and we are stemming the tide of expenditures and making Longbourn more profitable. If you and Mary would stop growing up, in three years I might be able to provide you with a tidy sum when you marry."

"Papa!"

"No? You won't accommodate my request?" He smiled at her. "Then you must continue as you have and find someone who will love you for who you are and not what you bring to the table."

"I have no plans to marry."

They both stood and Papa folded her into a warm hug. She felt a feather light kiss touch the top of her forehead.

"Do not let past remembrances stop you from moving forward, my Kitty. Know that you have my blessing to be happy and if that includes a husband, then so be it." He moved away and sat behind his desk once more. He picked up a sealed letter and handed it to her. "Here is a letter for your Uncle Gardiner. I have been sending him money over the past few months anticipating a time when you or Mary traveled to London and there is enough for you both to buy as many dresses and slippers as you want."

"Oh, Papa!" Kitty took the letter and leaned over to hug her father.

"There, there." He patted her arm which was wrapped around his shoulders. "You shall get my favorite coat all wet with tears. There's a good girl."

She straightened, but not before dropping a kiss on the top of his head. Before he could tease her for being a silly girl, she hurried from the room.

All too soon, the time for Lord George's arrival approached. Both she and Mary sat in the front parlor where they had an unobstructed view of the road. A clattering of hooves and the unmistakable sound of equipage pulling up had them rush to the window. Mouths slightly open in awe, they watched as four matching grays pulling an opulent carriage turned down their graveled drive. Behind them Lord George cantered on top of Buttons.

For one brief moment, Kitty felt a pinch of regret and turned from the window. Lord George had no intention of riding in the carriage with them. Silently she chastised herself. What made her think he'd lower himself to ride with two country girls with whom he had nothing in common?

"Girls! Lord Kerr has arrived. Come quickly," Mama called from the vestibule.

Both she and Mary grimaced, knowing how their mother's voice carried. Kitty hoped the equipage hadn't come to a complete stop as the sound of crunching gravel would cover the unladylike screeching of their mother.

"Mrs. Bennet. I pray you lower your voice. All of Meryton need not be advised of Lord George's arrival."

Papa had emerged from his book room and stood glaring at Mama. Suitably chastised, she smoothed down her skirts and in a more modulated voice, began again.

"Lord Kerr is here. I'll advise Hill to have Tom take out your trunks." With a flounce of her skirts, Mama turned toward the kitchen. To her surprise, Papa laughed and she stopped to glare at him. "You find humor in me, Mr. Bennet?"

"Nay, Mrs. Bennet. It is just that you reminded me of Lydia with your air of righteous indignation, even though you were in the wrong."

"Oh, how you vex me."

"Yes, and I take an uncommon delight in vexing you." He turned his focus onto his daughters. "Let us go greet the young man. He must be in want of a bracing cup of tea after riding all this way from Cambridgeshire."

Kitty followed Papa outside and watched as Lord George slid off Buttons and handed the reins to Hill's youngest boy who helped in the stable. Her throat tightened and her heart fluttered in her chest like a trapped bird as she took in his appearance. From his well-cut riding jacket down to his fawn colored breaches tucked into sturdy Hessian boots, he looked every inch the son of a Duke. The only thing which refused to conform was his hair. He'd removed his hat to give them a polite bow and one unruly lock of hair dared to fall across his forehead. It made him seem more human and the tightness in her throat lessened.

"Mr. Bennet. Miss Bennet, Miss Catherine." He greeted them all. When Mama burst through the door, he also gave her a polite bow. "Mrs. Bennet."

"Oh, Lord Kerr, how delightful to see you again. Would you like a cup of tea before you continue your journey?"

Mama, in spite of all her nervous fluttering and spasms, was renown by all as a gracious hostess.

"Alas, Mrs. Bennet, we must be away. I have urgent business in London and as such cannot tarry. Please accept my apologies and I promise the next time I am at Longbourn, I shall partake in a cup of tea with you."

Kitty thought Mama was about to faint dead away. However, she rallied and began directing where the trunks should be placed on the opulent carriage. The bitter side of Kitty wondered if she wanted her and Mary off as quickly as possible so she could visit their aunt in Meryton and gloat how Lord Kerr said he'd return for a visit.

What a kettle of worms he'd opened with one innocent remark. When he failed to keep that promise, she'd be the one to bear the brunt of her mother's displeasure. Just then a stable hand returned with Buttons, who'd been brushed down and given water.

"Well, girls, come give your Papa a proper hug, and remember to listen to your Aunt and Uncle Gardiner."

She and Mary hugged Papa and then Mama, who by this time had come to stand beside their father. She was surprised to see tears forming in their mother's eyes.

"Goodbye, Mama. I shall write often," Kitty whispered as she kissed her mother's cheek.

Lord George first offered his hand to Mary and once she was settled, turned toward Kitty. He helped her up into the carriage and she couldn't help but notice his hand lingered longer than was necessary on the small of her back. A tiny frisson of warmth crept through her body, which she immediately crushed. Having fanciful dreams about the handsome Lord was one thing, to act upon them was quite another.

No. She intended to maintain a polite civility between them, for when they arrived in London, he'd remain among his own set and forget the two lowly misses from Hertfordshire. Of that she was positive.

GEORGE SWUNG UP INTO the saddle and cursed his momentary lapse of judgement. Given the blush on Catherine's cheeks, she was very much aware his hand had lingered on the small of her back longer than propriety allowed. He had to give her time to become used to him, much like breaking in a new filly. You first started with a light blanket and slowly progressed to a saddle.

He waved a salute to their parents and Mrs. Bennet began waving a lacy handkerchief at the carriage as it trundled down the graveled drive. Both girls leaned out the window and waved back, only retreating to the interior when they turned onto the main road and moved out of sight of Longbourn.

He was most anxious to contact Lord Grayson and hand over the damning documents found in Stanhope's study. He'd deduced the initials S.P. stood for Spencer Percival, the Prime Minister who'd been assassinated. All along he'd felt there was a conspiracy behind Spencer's untimely death, now he had irrevocable proof. But more disturbing were the initials P.W., which had been stroked out. This led him to believe P.W. had been the original target and something happened to change the conspirator's plans.

If it had been just him and Buttons, he'd have ridden as though the hounds of hell were on his heels, but because of a promise and the very need to maintain the facade of a gentleman with no care, he had to bide his time. Hopefully, if the roads remained clear, he might catch Lord Grayson before he quit his offices for the evening. If not, then George might have to disturb him at home. Not only was the information he held vital, the life of the Prince Regent depended on finding Stanhope's alliance of traitors and bring them to justice.

Much to George's relief, there were no delays and they arrived on the outskirts of London in just under four hours. It took them another forty-five minutes to reach Gracechurch street, where Mrs. Bennet's brother resided in an elegant townhouse. Before the carriage had rolled to a complete stop, he jumped off Buttons and awaited the outrider to open the carriage door so he could help the ladies disembark.

Mary emerged first, thanking him in a most proper tone, followed by Catherine, her features hidden by the brim of her bonnet. She also murmured a polite thank you and went to step around him. An insane desire to tear the bonnet from her head and tilt up her face so he could see her eyes, consumed him. What would his Catherine do if he followed through?

She stumbled slightly and without thought he grabbed her arm and steadied her. Immediately she gasped and looked up. Her eyes were rounded in dismay and twin flags of red emblazoned her cheek. It was then he realized that he'd also wrapped his arm around her middle to keep her from falling. He released her and took a step back.

"My apologies, Miss Catherine. I did not want you to fall and re-injure your ribs."

While true, he knew he'd overstepped. His apology was cut short when the door to the townhouse opened. A portly man in his mid-thirties and a genteel looking woman descended the stairs and greeted both girls with a warm hug. He recalled seeing them at Darcy's wedding breakfast and also remembered how well-behaved their children had been.

"Uncle Gardiner, this is Lord George Kerr," Mary said by way of introduction.

The gentleman bowed in greeting and then brought forward his wife. "Yes, we met very briefly at Lizzy's wedding. This is my wife, Mrs. Gardiner."

She curtsied and George nodded in response.

"Thank you for escorting the girls, Lord Kerr. It is most appreciated." She nodded at the footmen to bring in the trunks. "After such a long journey, you must be in want of a good cup of tea. Would you join us, Lord Kerr?"

Her voice was low and soothing, her manner very welcoming. He could see why the sisters held her in such esteem.

"Yes, I would, although I can only stay for a quarter of an hour. I have a business engagement that cannot be put off any longer."

"Well, fortunately for you, Cook has everything prepared. All that is required is a dry mouth and empty stomach."

Catherine and Mary followed them into the house, disappearing upstairs to remove their traveling cloaks and freshen up. Excited squeals from the Gardiner children tumbled down the stairs and he was sure the two sisters were on the receiving end of some excited hugs. He followed Mrs. Gardiner into the front parlor. The room, although simply furnished, remained elegant. Compared to Adborough Hall, or even Kerr House it was small by comparison, but he liked how much it felt like a home. He settled into a comfortable chair beside the deep bay window and accepted a cup of tea from Mrs. Gardiner.

"Tell me, Lord Kerr, how you came to escort our nieces today." Mr. Gardiner lifted his cup of hot cocoa and blew across the steaming mug before taking a careful sip.

"It all began when I nearly ran over your niece, Miss Catherine..."

He had just finished relaying his story when Mary entered the room. Of their own accord, his gaze moved past her in anticipation of Catherine joining them. When she didn't appear, he turned his attention to Mary.

"Kitty has decided to remain upstairs, Aunt Gardiner. When she alighted from the carriage, she re-twisted her ankle and as such is laying down with it elevated, as Mr. Wilson prescribed."

"Is there anything I can do for her, Mr. Gardiner? Shall I call my family physician to attend?" George worked hard to show only light concern. As it was, he desperately wanted to take the stairs two at a time and see for himself that she was not badly re-injured.

"Thank you, but that is not necessary," Mr. Gardiner replied. "Given what Mary related in her letter to us last week, Kitty only requires a little rest and she shall be right as rain by tomorrow."

"Lord Kerr, you are so kind to offer us your own physician's assessment. However, you have more than made up for that unfortunate accident and simply must not take any more blame upon your shoulders." Mrs. Gardiner smiled at him.

The clock in the hall struck the quarter hour and George placed his tea back onto its dish and stood.

"I must be off. Please send my apologies to Miss Catherine and I hope she recovers quickly."

"We shall, Lord Kerr."

Mr. Gardiner accompanied him to the door and stayed on the front step as he swung up onto Buttons. The carriage and driver had already returned to Kerr House as planned and without further ado, he made his way to Lord Grayson's office.

TWO HOURS LATER, GEORGE rode a fatigued Buttons into the mews near his lodgings. Lord Grayson had already quit his office for the day, whereupon George attempted to speak with him at his house in Mayfair, only to find that his Lordship and wife were at Lady Dalrymple's ball.

Frustrated, George turned his faithful steed toward their own home and asked his valet, Mr. Pratt, to have a bath prepared. While soaking away over eight hours in the saddle he sat up with a splash and called for Pratt.

"Yes, Lord Kerr? Would you like to have some supper before retiring for the night?" he queried in his most polite tone.

"No, I mean I will have some supper, but I first need to know if any invitations to Lady Dalrymple's ball arrived for me."

"As a matter of fact, her invitation arrived the day you left for Cambridgeshire. I didn't mention it because you'd only just returned yourself, sir."

"No worries, Pratt. If you would set out my evening clothes and meet me in my dressing room. I am in need of a shave as well."

"Very good, my Lord. Do you require assistance getting out of the tub?"

"No, that will be all."

In no time, he was clean shaven, dressed in his finest evening wear with a pristine cravat so intricately knotted Brummel would gnash his teeth in envy, and his stomach had been soothed by a plate of meat and cheese Cook sent up to his room. Now all he had to do was locate Lord Grayson and tell him verbally about the evidence he had locked up in his strongbox.

Chapter Nine

"A message has arrived, ma'am."

"Did the messenger request a reply?" Aunt Gardiner asked as she accepted the sealed missive from their footman.

"No, ma'am." He bowed politely and left the room.

Kitty, Mary and Aunt Gardiner had just gathered together to break their fast in the room overlooking their Aunt's sumptuous flower garden. Uncle Gardiner, who'd eaten earlier, was already at his place of business. Both girls watched Aunt Gardiner break the seal and read the missive before placing the folded document beside her plate.

"Lord George Kerr is a most amiable man, would you not agree, Kitty?"

Caught unaware by the random question, Kitty almost spluttered out her tea.

"Yes... Yes, he is," she replied and quickly wiped her mouth with a linen handkerchief.

"And feels a great amount of guilt over your injuries, I would imagine," her aunt continued.

"I would not know, Aunt Gardiner. We have not spoken of it. In fact, we hardly have any sort of conversation. Ever."

"I find that interesting. He has requested to escort you and Mary to a few shops where you might buy gifts for your family and if there is time, show you Hyde Park. He will be here by one o'clock." Aunt Gardiner tapped the folded letter by her plate. "He is either a first-class gentleman, or a notorious rake, although he promised you will be suitably chaperoned. I am of a mind to consult your Uncle before making my decision."

"Whatever you think is best." Mary finally broke her silence, although her hand touched Kitty's leg under the table. A sign of silent support.

"I shall be but a few moments and I know your Uncle will respond quickly, as time is of the essence." Aunt Gardiner rose from the table and made her way to their Uncle's study.

"What do you make of that?" Mary asked Kitty once their aunt had quit the room.

"I hardly know. Why would he want to escort us shopping?"

Mary looked at her as though she suddenly had two heads instead of one.

"If you cannot comprehend the reason, then you are a dunderhead."

"Mary!" Kitty couldn't help herself, she laughed out loud. "You have become positively heathen in your language these past few days. I think I have become a bad influence on you."

"You would only be a bad influence if I spoke untruths, but in this - you are a dunderhead. You should have seen how crestfallen he was when you did not come downstairs after our arrival."

"I find that hard to believe. I think you are looking for roses where only bright weeds grow."

She wouldn't allow Mary's verbal musings to turn her head, she performed that task all on her own. During their uneventful trip to London she'd caught glimpses of him riding beside the carriage. He seemed as one with his horse, muscular thighs hugging the saddle, hands loose on the reins. He'd been so incredibly male, so masculine that she couldn't help but stare until she realized Mary watched her almost as close as she watched him. After that she'd kept her attention firmly inside the carriage.

He was only being a gentleman and now that they were in London it was only natural he would ease out of their lives into his own. His singular attention had been flattering, but she had no expectations of something further. She repeated 'no expectations' to herself, almost as a mantra. Maybe if she whispered it enough times, she'd come to believe it.

Within the hour their Uncle responded with permission for them to be escorted by Lord Kerr and to have their own maid, Nanette, attend them.

Now, at precisely ten minutes to one o'clock, her heart pounded so hard Mary was sure to hear the panicked thump, thump, thump from where she sat embroidering. Kitty fought the urge to pace the room, or worse, stand by the window and watch for his arrival.

"Kitty. Your behavior reminds me of a cat inside a room full of dogs. Even from here I can see how tight your nerves are stretched."

"I am worried Aunt and Uncle Gardiner will think there is a secret understanding between Lord George and me. Although I anticipate with pleasure seeing all the shops and maybe also Hyde Park, I debate whether I should decline his gracious invitation"

"Have you gone completely mad?" Mary lowered the embroidery hoop onto her lap, her expression incredulous. "Why would you decline Lord Kerr's invitation, and even more perplexing, what is wrong with him showing you attention? He is the brother of a Duke! Hundreds of young women covet his attention, of this I am positive."

"It is not that simple. I cannot... I... He must not pay so much attention to me." She trained her eyes onto her hands, clasped tightly on her lap. "If he is in search of a bride, he should not waste time with us."

The sound of a carriage arriving halted their conversation. Mary placed her work into a handy little box beside the couch and Kitty took a deep, fortifying breath. Soon the sounds of Lord George being welcomed by their Uncle could be heard. He'd returned home in time to greet the young gentleman.

"Kitty." Mary commanded her attention before their company joined them. "Put that heavy burden down. You promised."

Surprised tears threatened to appear. How wonderful her sister was. Mary promised to help her let go of her dark past and this proved she was a woman of her word. She smiled and willed the tears to abate.

"Thank you, Mary. I need your calming influence."

"And some of Lizzy's courage."

She felt a rush of longing for the company of her sisters. Lizzy always had courage when facing the unknown and Jane accepted everything with calm serenity while Lydia surged ahead, sails fully extended uncaring what course her ship took.

"I just realized something." Kitty said with a little laugh. "Between us five sisters, we have a perfect woman."

"What on earth do you mean?"

"Well... Jane has a sweet temper, Lizzy has courage which rises to every occasion, you have good morals, Lydia has boundless enthusiasm and love of all things fun, and I have loyalty."

"I never thought of us that way," Mary laughed with her. "That is absolutely brilliant."

"What is brilliant, Mary?" their aunt asked, entering the room before the gentleman joined them.

"Not what, but who. My sister, Catherine. She is an absolute gem."

"I have always known she is a treasure, as are you, Mary." Her aunt gave them a sweet smile.

"Thank you, Aunt," both girls spoke in unison.

"Ladies, are you ready for your afternoon jaunt?" their uncle asked as he entered the room, followed by Lord George who looked more handsome than ever, if that were possible.

His well-cut maroon jacket appeared to have been molded to his form and her greedy eyes traveled down taking in every detail. Unruly curls, broad shoulders, a cravat so intricately knotted she wondered how long it took his valet to execute the knots and turns, down past his tan waistcoat and fawn colored breeches tucked into expensive boots. Everything about him shouted to the world he was a gentleman of the ton, a titled brother to a Peer of the realm.

He was beyond the boundaries of her world.

⟜⟡⟝

"A BOOKSTORE! I HAVE always wanted to see one." Kitty eagerly scanned the interior of the shop through the window.

Lord George had taken them down a small side street, just off the main road. At first trepidation filled her, thinking he didn't want to be seen with her and Mary by anyone of Quality, but then he stopped in front of a delightful bookstore, tucked away like a happy secret.

"You have never been to a bookstore?" Lord George's voice was incredulous.

"No, all we have in Meryton is the circulating library. If we want anything special, we have to order it from Town." She gazed longingly at all the books on display. Mary stood quietly beside her, also gazing at the books.

"Then we must go in."

"Oh no," both girls said at the same time. Kitty felt her cheeks heat in shame. How does one tell a handsome lord, a rich handsome lord, that neither she nor Mary could scarce afford to purchase a new book? No, they would have to carry on to the park as planned.

"Might I enquire why, when the door to the building is neither locked nor barred to female customers?" Lord George's habitual grin graced his face again, his dimple deepening.

"We do not have funds to purchase anything," Mary stated in her matter-of-fact way and Kitty wished she were anywhere but here. "I cannot speak for my sister, but for me it would be heart wrenching to go inside and not indulge. Much like a child in a sweet shop."

Understanding dawned on Lord George's face. He carefully assessed each girl and Kitty knew exactly when he'd made a decision. His shoulders straightened and his chest even puffed out a bit. He was fascinating to watch and when he turned to face her, she blushed even further at being caught.

"Let me escort you inside. I insist on you buying anything you want."

"We cannot infringe upon you, Lord Kerr." Kitty protested. "You are neither a brother, nor other relation to us. It would seem most improper."

"Miss Catherine. Consider this as recompense for nearly killing you with my horse. In fact, I insist." He placed her gloved hand on his arm and proceeded to escort her and Mary into the shop. "One book for each of you."

At first all Kitty and Mary could do was stand in awe. The scent of old leather and dusty pages reminded Kitty of her father's book room. How he would love to wander the aisles and peruse the titles. She laughed softly. They'd never see their father at all if they brought him here.

"Is there anything special you would like, Miss Catherine?"

She gave a start when Lord George appeared by her side. Engrossed with the plethora of books around her, she'd almost forgotten about him. She cut a glance at him from beneath the brim of her bonnet, strangely pleased to find him close, his eyes twinkling as though he knew what a treat this was. His dimple appeared again as he smiled down at her. Really, he smiled too much. It was hard to read his character when he always appeared so congenial, much like Charles, Jane's new husband.

"Oh no. I do not want anything for myself."

"But, I insist. You cannot leave the store without a book in your hand."

Kitty frowned. It was most improper for Lord George to purchase a book for an unmarried woman who was not family. She dared to look at him again and laughed softly.

Lord George was giving her a most mournful look, almost pleading.

"You look like one of Papa's hounds when they want the juiciest bone to chew."

"Are you saying I look like a dog?" Lord George stepped back in mock horror and Kitty laughed out loud when he clutched his heart.

"Stop. It is most unladylike to laugh in a bookstore." She covered her mouth with her hand and turned to hide her smile.

"I am most wounded. I shall have to tell your father how you cut me through with your cruel words."

"Papa would applaud my behavior. He is a great study of character and loves all things absurd." Kitty sniffed and tilted her nose in a teasing manner. "No, if you truly wish to make me pay for bad behavior, you must tell Mama. She would have the appropriate fits and vapors to satisfy your ungentlemanlike behavior."

Lord George drew near to her again and leaned in. "Very well, Miss Catherine," he whispered in her ear, "You give me no choice. I ride to Longbourn tonight. What say you now?"

"You do that, Lord George." She moved down the aisle, away from his disturbing presence. "Please give my parents my warmest regard."

She met up with Mary who was perusing a slim volume of poems. Mary glanced past her shoulder, back to the area where she'd left Lord George standing.

"What did you say to Lord Kerr?" Mary whispered and turned her attention back to the book.

"Nothing much, really. He was being a pest." She moved closer to Mary and whispered, "Why do you ask? What is he doing now?"

"I refuse to be drawn into childish parlor games being played out in a public venue." At Kitty's plea of, 'Mary!', she relented. "He watched you walk away with a look of admiration. Whatever you said pleased him."

"May I help you ladies find a particular book?"

The clerk had approached them and Mary answered with a polite smile. "Yes, please. I am looking for the novel, *Sense and Sensibility*, written by A Lady."

"I know exactly which book you speak of." With a flourish of his arm, he bade Kitty and Mary to follow him.

Lord George approached again.

"Miss Catherine, are you sure I cannot entice you to buy something for yourself?"

"No, thank you." She paused as an idea entered her mind. "Could I purchase something for my father? There is a book he has always wanted. He misses our sister Elizabeth so much, this might cheer him up."

"Most assuredly. I think that is a wonderful idea."

Kitty hurried to the counter, near the front of the store.

"Have you decided which book you would like, Miss?" the clerk queried.

"Yes. Do you have any first editions of *Robinson Crusoe*?"

"I might have one copy in the back." He peered over the rim of his spectacles at her. "The weather has been fine this year."

"If you were a duck, perhaps, but I prefer long sun-filled days." Kitty bestowed a small smile upon the clerk, very aware Lord George lurked a few bookshelves away. "When I anticipate the warm months approaching I think of Shakespeare, who wrote, 'Shall I compare thee to a summer's day?'

Would Lord George be impressed by her knowledge of the bard's work? She cast a furtive glance at him and wondered at the dark scowl creasing his forehead. Stupid, stupid pride. What had she been thinking? She faced the clerk and clasped her shaking hands.

The clerk excused himself and disappeared behind a curtain. Within a few minutes he returned with a leather-bound edition of *Robinson Crusoe*. He began to wrap the book in plain brown paper while Mary came alongside and placed a few books on the counter.

"I see you have found some more novels. Will they fill the 'hidden depths' of your soul, dear sister?" Kitty teased, referencing the hollowed-out tome where Mary hid her books.

"There is so much to choose from, I can scarce bring myself to leave." Mary graced her with a wide smile and opened her reticule in preparation to pay for her books. Kitty knew she'd earmarked this money for some new music sheets and felt a pang of regret at her sister having to choose one enjoyment over another. However, this wasn't the first time a Bennet girl had sacrificed because of no money. With a mother who didn't budget and always had a thin purse, they'd all, with the exception of Lydia, learned to economize.

She reached for her own reticule, determined to give Mary the money she'd won from Papa when Lord George stepped forward.

"Put your money away, Miss Bennet. Remember, I promised to pay for your purchases in recompense for my reckless behavior." He glanced at the clerk and asked in what Kitty thought was a somewhat foppish voice. "How much for these young lady's books?"

The clerk told him the amount and her stomach plummeted.

"Sir, I cannot have you spend such a large amount on my sister and me. This is beyond the pale."

"Nonsense. I insist." Lord George pulled out some bank notes and with a flourish counted off three. "There you are my good man. Can you please wrap up the other young lady's books as well?"

While he tucked the remaining bank notes into his coat pocket, the clerk wrapped up Mary's books. Within minutes the three of them were back on the street and Lord George returned to his normal, cheerful self.

"Now, I insist on treating you all to an iced treat at Gunter's."

He took each of them by the arm and strolled back toward the main road, stopping at a lively shop where customers sat at small tables, enjoying a multitude of treats. Kitty wondered why he had portrayed himself in such a silly manner inside the store. Instinctively she knew he'd behaved in that way so the clerk's attention would be drawn to him and not her and Mary. Was that because he was ashamed of them?

Her head began to ache from all the questions running around in her mind. Lord George was anything but dull. One minute flirtatious, the next scowling and the next a foppish fool. What was he like when he was alone and there was no one around to entertain? She shook her head. She'd never know. That privilege would belong to some other lady.

WHILE CATHERINE AND Miss Bennet enjoyed their iced treat, George analyzed the incident at the bookstore. Last night, prior to attending Lady Dalrymple's ball, he'd spoken with his man Henry, who'd been tasked with keeping an eye on Stanhope while George was out of town. Henry informed him that Stanhope attended this particular bookstore several times during the week, always leaving with a scowl upon his face.

Curious to the nature of Stanhope's activities, George escorted the Miss Bennet's there in hopes of uncovering something, without even knowing what exactly to look for. The exchange which transpired between Miss Catherine and the clerk came as a complete surprise. Having been in covert operations for over five years, he immediately recognized the gambit when the clerk asked Catherine about the weather.

If she answered correctly, he would pass information to her via the book. If incorrect, she would leave the store none the wiser, thinking there were no first edition books of Robinson Crusoe at this particular shop.

Obviously, quoting Shakespeare was the appropriate response. He already knew the Viscount was a traitor to England, but this new piece of evidence might lead him to Stanhope's contact in France, or at least give him a working knowledge of how he passed information. When Stanhope realized someone other than himself was in possession of his book, he'd be relentless in his pursuit. It was imperative he re-visit Lord Grayson and fill him in on what he'd learned today.

CATHERINE

While the Misses Bennet enjoyed their ices, he took time to appraise them both. Although in a much lighter mood than he'd observed at Longbourn, Miss Bennet continued to be more reserved than her sister. Her eyes remained lowered and she didn't attempt to look around and watch the other patrons. Catherine on the other hand continually twisted in her seat. She had an eye for fashion and when a lady went by wearing an outrageous hat, her eyes lit up and she raised a gloved hand to hide a smile. She then leaned toward Miss Bennet and soon her sister's gaze followed the bobbing ostrich feather which adorned the monstrous bonnet.

"Who is wearing who?" she asked Catherine.

That was when he knew Miss Mary Bennet had a hidden intelligence and was not the quiet mouse everyone assumed. Catherine smothered a laugh and glanced in his direction. Her bright eyes danced with amusement and she tried valiantly to maintain calm and composure, but her lips kept twitching.

It was then the hat changed direction, came into the shop and toward their table. The two girls' eyes widened in horror when they realized the woman was almost upon them. Miss Bennet and Catherine exchanged glances, most likely fearing the woman heard Miss Bennet's comment. He noted they held hands beneath the table and was warmed by their act of solidarity.

He didn't fear for the Bennet sisters as he knew to whom the hat belonged – Evangeline in all her glory – accompanied by her companion, Miss Bledsoe. He was a bit surprised to see the young woman as George could not recall when, if ever, he'd seen her outside of Evangeline's home.

George stood, in anticipation of introducing the Countess and her companion to the two young ladies from Hertfordshire. However, neither of them anticipated Catherine's reaction, who rose to her feet and smiled at Miss Bledsoe walking a few paces behind Evangeline.

"Lady Harriet!" she exclaimed.

All color fled from Miss Bledsoe's face and she stopped cold in her tracks. Names, faces and information George had gleaned over the past week began to click into place.

"Lord George." Evangeline cried out and surged forward, concealing her companion who turned and fled the shop. "I am pleased to see you."

Catherine's gaze rose upward to the bobbing ostrich feather. Familiar with Evangeline's foibles and eccentricities, he knew beyond a shadow of doubt her goal was to divert Catherine's attention from Miss Bledsoe to herself. He steeled himself to remain calm at her subterfuge as Evangeline would know immediately if something was amiss, but his pulse raced and his thoughts shot off like a startled horse.

Had Catherine inadvertently stumbled upon a connection between Stanhope and the botched burglary? Everything in him clamored to follow Miss Bledsoe as she slipped across the street and melted into the shadows between shops. Instead he gave Evangeline a small bow of his head.

"May I introduce Miss Bennet and Miss Catherine Bennet of Longbourn. And this is my good friend, Lady Evangeline Cavendish, Countess of Anstruther."

Miss Bennet gave a polite nod.

"Good afternoon, Countess." Catherine said and performed a quick curtsy. "I apologize for my atrocious manners.

For a brief moment I thought your companion was a childhood friend, Lady Harriet Jacobson. Someone I have not seen in ten years."

"Impossible. Miss Bledsoe has been my companion for over five years," Evangeline pronounced in a firm voice. "I know everything there is about her background and heritage. However, everyone has a doppelganger, and she must be your friend's."

Evangeline turned her attention back to George, all charm and good humor, but he knew Catherine's observation had rattled her. He pulled out the remaining chair and the Countess lowered herself with careless grace. Catherine seated herself at a much slower pace, her countenance still revealing confusion.

"Lord George, have you spoken with our mutual acquaintance and been successful in your..." Evangeline paused for a dramatic moment, fluttering her hand back and forth in front of her face as though searching for the word. "Ah, yes. Success in your quest?"

George did not answer right away. Several avenues of thought raced through his brain as he continued to piece together disjointed information and scenes. The peculiar sense that he'd recognized Stanhope's daughter from the miniature became clear. One, she'd been considerably younger and didn't have her disfiguring scar at the time the portrait had been painted, and two, no one expected to find a Viscount's only daughter employed as a paid companion to the eccentric Countess of Anstruther.

More disturbing thoughts filled him with unease. Had Evangeline killed the valet in order to silence him? Was she a double agent, equally exposing English secrets to France, to the point of jeopardizing the safety of her own husband? Was Stanhope's daughter the hidden connection? Even more disconcerting was the fact that Miss Catherine Bennet knew Miss Bledsoe, or rather, Lady Harriet by sight.

As much as he ached to analyze all aspects of what just occurred, this was neither the time nor place. His only solution was to slip into the persona of a carefree man in the delightful company of three ladies. However, until he knew exactly where Evangeline fit into all of this, and because of the presence of two young ladies from Hertfordshire, he'd couch his replies in general terms. As far as he knew, Evangeline had no knowledge of his trip to Cambridgeshire.

"My quest never bore fruit, I'm afraid. Instead, I traveled to my estate in Cambridgeshire, which has been sadly neglected and have begun making amends to the staff by hiring a new housekeeper. I'm sure she shall have Keswick Manor up and running within the month."

Evangeline tinkled out a light laugh. "Lord George, I cannot imagine you living the life of a country gentleman. However, you have surprised me more than once in all the years we have known each other."

"How long have you known each other, Countess Anstruther?"

Miss Bennet's quiet voice carried over the din in the shop. Evangeline twisted a bit on her chair and smiled at her.

"I have known Lord George for many years but we only recently re-connected when I returned to England from the Continent at one of Lady Miranda Blake's afternoon soirees. He was there with his lovely mother, the Dowager Duchess, and quickly became a friendly face in the crowd."

"How frightening that must have been, to be on the Continent during these dangerous times." Catherine clasped Mary's hand again. "You are so brave."

Evangeline reached out and placed her gloved hand over the two sister's hands.

"We must pray hard for England's shores to remain safe. I have many friends who are still trapped in France and until that little man is removed, I will have no rest." She released their hands and dug out a lacy handkerchief from her reticule and dabbed gently around her eyes. Once they were dried she rose to her feet and George quickly stood.

"Enough tears over my heartache. No more." She tucked the handkerchief back into her bag and faced him. "I have many more engagements before the day ends. It was lovely to meet such fine young ladies from Hertfordshire, and also to see you again, Lord George."

He took her hand and bowed low. Upon him releasing her fingers, she turned and with a lilting 'Good day', exited the shop. He watched her cross the street toward a carriage stopped in front of a milliner's shop. Miss Bledsoe slipped out of the alleyway and quickly ascended into its interior after Evangeline.

It was only after he dropped off the Bennet sisters at their Aunt and Uncle's home in Cheapside, and was alone in his carriage, that he opened the note Evangeline pressed into his hand before taking her leave.

Chapter Ten

"Who is Lady Harriet?" Mary asked once she and Kitty returned to their Aunt and Uncle Gardiner's home and were alone in Kitty's room.

"Lady Harriet is the only daughter of Viscount Stanhope."

"Are you positive it was her? It must have been over ten years since you visited with Papa. I remember as it was the year Lydia had those dreadful spots and fever and Mama insisted he take you with him."

"It was ten years ago, and yes, the Countess' maid is Lady Harriet. Although much altered, I would recognize those green eyes anywhere, plus she has a scar at the top of her lip. I remember it being quite ugly and raw when I last saw her." Kitty shuddered at the memory and sat on the edge of her bed. "Why would she pretend to be a companion? She is an English lady, born and bred and her family is not destitute. Her father is very much alive."

"She must have her reasons and it is not our secret to give away."

"Oh, Mary, I am tired of keeping so many secrets."

"Other than Lydia's previous behavior and Janes' suspected pregnancy, what secrets do you harbor?"

Ice cold fear sliced through Kitty's veins. How could she have slipped up like that? No one, other than Papa knew of her secret. Seeing Lady Harriet had brought back a lot of memories she'd rather not dwell upon. Memories which would awaken her in the night and she'd not experienced those night horrors in many years.

"Things, like Mama sending too much money to Lydia, or you hiding scurrilous books in Fordyce's Sermons that would cause Mr. Collins to have an apoplectic fit," she hedged, not willing to say anything further.

"Those are not big secrets, Kitty. It is not like you have killed someone and hidden their body." Mary paused and peered at her in concern. "You haven't killed someone and hidden the body, have you?"

"Oh, my goodness," she laughed out. "Who in the world would I murder? We must stop reading those horrible books filled with mystery and murder. They make our thoughts wander down paths that are ridiculous."

Mary laughed with her. "You are right. For a brief moment you seemed so sincere, as though you had a secret which weighed you down like a mill stone."

How astute her sister was and Kitty longed to divulge her secret and have someone to share the pain and humiliation that rested solely on her shoulders. Papa knew, but other than the one brief moment before their last dinner at Longbourn, he never once alluded to, nor acknowledged that horrible night. Instead, he hid away in his book room, acting as though her world had not fallen to pieces.

In some ways she missed the man Papa had been. Gregarious by nature, he'd welcomed friends and family into their home and regaled them all with stories of his youth. The house was filled with music and laughter and Fanny Bennet rejoiced in the role of hostess. Papa stayed in contact with his Cambridge friends until one in particular invited him for a shooting party. Kitty attended because of Lydia's malaise, plus the man had a daughter the same age and they would entertain each other. Her excitement knew no bounds, but neither of them expected the horrors that followed them home. Laughter fled Longbourn, never to return.

"Kitty, are you all right?" Mary leaned closer to look her in the eye. "You have become so quiet."

She picked up the ribbon from her bonnet, smoothing the blue velvet before hanging it on a little wire placed beside the bed. "I am well. Just wool gathering, as Lizzy would say."

"Lady Harriet aside, what did you think of Lady Evangeline's hat?"

"Absolutely hideous! I worried a live ostrich would leap off her head and chase us down the street." She shook her head at the memory.

"Stop," Mary laughed out, holding her sides. "My stomach hurts from laughing so much."

"Girls?"

Kitty and Mary stopped laughing and turned toward the door, where their Aunt stood.

"Aunt Gardiner, we were talking about a hat we saw."

"Do you not think that's cruel? To ridicule someone's choice of millinery?"

Their Aunt advanced into the room and stood before them, a slight frown on her forehead. Kitty started to reassure her that she and Mary weren't trying to be cruel, but Mary forestalled her comment by saying, "If you had seen this bonnet, you also would have questioned the lady's choice of apparel, for never have I seen a hat wear a woman!"

Kitty and Mary burst into laughter again and their Aunt watched them, a smile tugging at her lips.

"Was it really that bad?"

"Yes!" Kitty patted the bed between her and Mary, inviting their Aunt to sit. "Join us and we shall tell you all about the Countess of Anstruther's fantastic hat."

GEORGE STARED INTO the fire, a glass of hot apple cider in his hand. The flickering flames normally calmed his spirits but tonight, they licked at his memories and stirred up disturbing images.

Back and forth, his train of thought vacillated. He trusted Evangeline. They'd been through too much both in France and England for him to doubt her constancy, yet Stanhope's daughter was her companion and confidant. This business with Miss Bledsoe placed a different spin on things and his sense of urgency increased at the content of the note Evangeline pressed into his hand.

> *I find I must make an arduous voyage to visit mutual friends on the Continent. I have received disturbing news they have experienced unusual difficulties, which explains why I have not heard from them these past few months. I pray I find them safe and that nothing untoward has happened and will pass along your warm regard when I see them.*

Yours, etc.,

E.C.

George knew that Evangeline had couched her information in general terms, on the off chance someone other than himself gained access to her note, but he knew she'd passed plenty of information in these few lines.

She was on her way to France to contact their courier, whom she hadn't heard from in a while. That by itself was troubling, but it could also mean their contact had been compromised, which in turn meant her husband could also be in peril.

The note, and the knowledge that Catherine was in possession of a book he knew Stanhope coveted and would soon discover missing, made him long to pace the room – again. He rubbed his lower lip. Somehow, he had to gain possession of that book.

He picked up the small pile of invitations his butler had laid on the corner of the desk and began to sort through them. Most found their way into the rubbish bin, but one. He stared at the handwritten invitation to his brother's engagement dinner, slated for the following Thursday at Kerr House.

Given that he and his brothers were still in half mourning for Uncle Moreland, the dinner would be a small affair for close family and friends only. Charles Bingley and his wife Jane would be in attendance, as well as Mr. and Mrs. Darcy, who were travelling down from Pemberley for the occasion. Tomorrow he'd stop by Kerr House and make sure the invitation included four more family members, for surely Max wouldn't exclude two of the former Miss Bennet's sisters and well as their much beloved Aunt and Uncle Gardiner. From there, he'd find a way to secure Miss Catherine's book as well as enjoy her enchanting personality.

"WHAT BRINGS YOU TO Kerr House so early in the morning?" Max laid the morning paper down beside his plate when George entered the sunny breakfast room of Kerr House.

"Can I not come and enjoy your sumptuous fare? Must I await an invitation?"

George moved to the sideboard and helped himself to a platter of crisp bacon, a fresh scone and a spoonful of eggs. As he seated himself to the right of Max, a diligent footman poured him a cup of tea.

"You know you do not need an invitation. Kerr House is your home as well. I am still perplexed as to the reasons why you keep a separate apartment. Such a waste of money."

"A man needs privacy, Max." George grinned at the frown that marred his elder brother's face. "Not for what you think, but to have a space that is all my own. I love you and Mother, but I need to be my own man."

"I suppose this is why you have decided to take up Mother's offer of Keswick Manor?"

"It is. I have just returned from Cambridgeshire and advised the staff."

"Mmmm... yes. Mother received notice from Mrs. Walbush. You will have to find a replacement."

"Already taken care of. Do you remember Mr. Power?"

"Our vicar?"

"Yes, in a strange sequence of events, I met his daughter. She is widowed with two children and in need of employment."

"Is that not a tad presumptuous, offering such a responsible job to someone so young?"

"Not at all." George wiped his mouth with a fresh linen napkin. "Her husband was deployed to the war and died four years ago. She has been serving as one of the primary maids in a country house nearby." He laid the napkin down. "Given that we can vouch for her history and good moral standing, and the fact that she is well aware of how a house is run, I saw this as a perfect opportunity to raise her family's standard of living."

"You said she was in need of employment, yet you said she had been in a household for over four years. Was she fired, and if yes, for what cause?"

Drat Maxwell and his analytical mind.

"I will not bore you with much detail, but the household she worked for was Stanhope's. I am sure you understand why I wish to remove our former vicar's daughter from the presence of that vile man."

Max's eyebrows raised slightly and he grimaced. "I understand completely but the role of a housekeeper has far more responsibility than a maid dusting furniture."

George gave his brother a disgusted look.

"I am not completely unaware and Mrs. Walbush has agreed to stay a few more months to ease her into the position. In fact, she is quite excited to begin training Mrs. Nelson."

He took care to use Mrs. Sheraton's new identity. Max had no requirement to know her name was a complete fabrication, or that Mrs. Walbush was in on the ruse.

"I pray this works out for all involved." Max cut into a piece of ham. "Stanhope's estate is not an ideal place for any woman of virtue to work at."

After enjoying the remainder of his sumptuous breakfast with Max, George directed a footman to deliver his card to the Gardiner residence, advising he would call later that day. He looked forward to seeing Catherine and also to gain custody of her father's new book.

"I WOULD LOVE TO SEE the book you bought for your father, Miss Catherine."

"I have not yet unwrapped it. I wish to leave the package as is until I present it to him." She twisted her fingers together in her lap. "I am sure you understand."

"I do, indeed. Pray do not worry yourself in this fashion." He gave a tiny smile and watched some of the tension leave her shoulders. "I shall pester your father when next I see him."

Careful not to display any frustration, he turned to Mrs. Gardiner, who'd watched their exchange with bright eyes. Although the Gardiner's manners were always pleasing, he knew they wondered at his attention to their niece.

"Mrs. Gardiner, my brother Maxwell is giving a dinner in honor of Nathan and Miss Bingley's engagement next Thursday. I know Mr. and Mrs. Darcy, as well as Mr. and Mrs. Bingley shall be attending. Because your family will be connected to ours, he has asked me to extend this invitation to you and your nieces."

Mrs. Gardiner's eyes widened in surprise and she paused in giving an answer, glancing over toward her husband. George understood her hesitation. It was not every day that a person associated with trade was invited to dine with a Duke.

Unspoken communication winged its way between the married couple and Mr. Gardiner responded. "We would be delighted, for nothing else but to see our happily married nieces."

"Excellent. May I send a carriage around to collect you?"

"Not necessary, Lord Kerr. I have my own conveyance."

Based on what he'd seen of their elegant home, he knew Mr. Gardiner had a thriving business, but to keep a carriage and horses meant Catherine's uncle was doing very well for himself. The better acquainted he became with her extended family, the more he liked them. It was such a pleasure to be appreciated solely for himself and not for what his status in Society.

"Then I look forward to Thursday evening. With the whole family there, it should be a lively affair."

"Yes, I cannot wait to see our Lizzy and Jane. They both write such beautiful letters, but it's not the same as speaking with them in person," Mrs. Gardiner said.

"I agree. Maxwell hides himself away at Adborough Hall for months on end and his correspondence is adequate, but I enjoy the comfort of his company far more than a letter."

KITTY COULD BARELY contain her excitement. Lizzy and Mr. Darcy, Jane and Mr. Bingley had arrived in London the night previous, and given the lateness of the hour decided not come to their Aunt's home for a much-needed visit. This would be the first time she'd seen her sisters since their weddings last

November. Six months was the longest amount of time they'd ever been apart.

In anticipation of Lizzy's arrival, she and Mary packed their trunks and Darcy's man had picked them up earlier in the afternoon. After dinner at the Duke of Adborough's, she and her sister would travel back to Darcy's house and stay there before heading North to Pemberley.

Sadly, Mary made the decision to return to Longbourn, much to Kitty's dismay. She'd come to appreciate Mary so much in the past few months and didn't want to lose this closeness they'd achieved, but her elder sister felt their mother needed her at home. Mama's letters had such an air of melancholy and they both agreed their mother was not used to a large, mostly silent house. Hopefully, Mary would fill the quiet with her music and soothe Mama's nerves. Something their father would be thankful for.

Finally, their carriage arrived at Kerr House. Prior to disembarking, Aunt Gardiner covered Kitty's hands with one of hers.

"Are you excited to see your sisters, or has someone else captured your attention?"

"Aunt Gardiner!" Kitty was glad the carriage lay in semi-darkness, hiding the blush she knew colored her cheeks.

"Are you coming, my dear?" Uncle Gardiner had helped Mary out of the carriage and now stood waiting for his wife and other niece.

"One moment." Aunt Gardiner fixed her attention to Kitty. "Although a fine young man, he is very experienced in the way of the world. I advise you to exercise caution. I am sorry I waited until now, but you were so busy packing I did not have time to discuss this earlier. I would not want you to give your heart without knowing the true man and what his intentions are."

"I have no expectations, Aunt. Lord George feels nothing more than friendship. I do not believe he has any regard for me – not in the way you intimate."

"I pray you are right." Aunt squeezed her hand. "Remember, you can always come to me if you have any questions or need to talk through a decision."

"Thank you. I know your instructions are always sound."

"My dear, the Duke is waiting." Uncle Gardiner's voice was tinged with the slightest hint of impatience.

"Yes, dear."

Aunt Gardiner accepted her husband's help out of the carriage. He then turned and handed Kitty down.

"After you, ladies."

Kitty stood in awe as she waited for her uncle to knock on the door. From the outside, Kerr House was an elegant structure with two large bay windows and a beautifully proportioned ionic portico. Her gaze climbed higher, across the neat, stuccoed façade to the impossible height of the roof. A fanciful thought of opening a window on the upper levels and reaching out to touch a cloud was interrupted by the opening of the massive walnut door.

The four of them entered the foyer, a gleaming expanse of white marble. A procession of gilt edged paintings marched up the sweeping staircase that curved out of sight to the first floor. It was down these stairs that the Duke of Adborough descended, followed by Lord George.

She wasn't sure if it was nothing more than wishful thinking, but it seemed as though Lord George's smile became a bit warmer when his gaze landed on her. To hide her sudden bout of nerves, she fussed with her spencer and gloves, handing them and her bonnet to a waiting footman.

"Welcome to Kerr House," the Duke said. "Darcy and Elizabeth have not yet arrived and Bingley and Jane have written to say they will be a little late. Shall we proceed to the drawing room and then George can properly introduce everyone."

The Duke's butler moved toward a double set of doors at Maxwell's slight nod of direction and opened them to a well-proportioned room, the walls a pleasing pale yellow. Comfortable settees and chairs were sprinkled about the room and a glossy pianoforte held court in the alcove which Kitty realized was one of the bay windows she'd seen from the street.

More gilt-edged paintings adorned the walls, although not as large as those in the foyer. The butler closed the door behind him and Lord George immediately began introductions.

"Mr. and Mrs. Edward Gardiner, Miss Bennet and Miss Catherine Bennet may I introduce you to my brother, Maxwell Kerr, the Fifth Duke of Adborough."

The women curtsied and Mr. Gardiner gave a respective bow, returned by a slight nod from the Duke.

"Nathan shall be down shortly, as soon as Miss Bingley arrives with her family. He only arrived late this afternoon and as such had to freshen up – considerably."

"Indeed," Lord George said with a laugh. "After three hard days on a horse, I advised him to soak for at least an hour."

Maxwell indicated for the butler to begin serving drinks.

"Mr. Gardiner, I have heard many good things about your acumen in business. I intend to pick your brain over some investments I am considering, as well as Darcy."

"I am but a simple business owner, Your Grace. I do not take unnecessary risks and choose my investments after careful consideration."

"Exactly the reason why I wish to confer with you. We will talk later and not bore the ladies with all of this." He turned his attention to Mrs. Gardiner. "Are you enjoying this time with your nieces."

From there the conversation turned to generalities, with the Duke encouraging Aunt Gardiner to regale him with stories of their four children. Kitty was astonished with how amiable the Duke was. They were agreeably engaged for about ten minutes when the butler opened the door to announce Mr. Darcy, Lizzy, Mr. Bingley, Jane and Miss Bingley. They'd barely set foot into the drawing room when Lord Nathan appeared, taking Miss Bingley's hand and tucking it onto his arm.

Kitty felt a sharp tug of envy at the look of adoration which crossed Miss Bingley's upturned face. That her love was returned by the handsome Lord Nathan was evidenced by the smile which softened his countenance. To have such love and know it was returned. Her chest constricted and without thought she rubbed at her chest, right above her heart. She'd give anything to freely love and be loved.

Chapter Eleven

George watched Catherine press her fingers above her heart, her eyes filled with such longing he almost crossed the room to ask what was wrong. Mindful of appearances he remained with Maxwell. Running to the side of an unmarried miss the minute she showed signs of distress would be as good as reading the banns. He liked Miss Catherine Bennet, of that he had no doubt, but he also had no immediate plans of announcing his intentions. They first needed to become better acquainted.

He knew she liked his attentions, that she looked forward to their excursions given the brightness of her eyes when they lit on him, but she remained as skittish as an unbroken filly. Dancing around their attraction, unwilling to let him close enough to capture her heart.

She remained an enigma, which was part of her charm. Miss Catherine Bennet didn't flirt, she didn't bat her eyes, she didn't try to contrive 'chance' meetings – instead she spoke honestly, averted her gaze when he flirted with her, and seemed genuinely pleased when he happened across them the other day when she and her sister were shopping with their Aunt.

One day, when they were old and gray, he'd confess how he had one of his footmen watch their Uncle's house and report where they'd gone. With Miss Catherine, he planned on leaving nothing to 'chance'.

"You and your bride are well?" George asked Darcy, when all the noise of greetings had finally abated.

"We are. I am a happily situated man."

"I thought you might have brought Georgiana with you this evening. I know she is not out yet, but this is a family dinner, of sorts."

"I dare say she would have come if she could. She has a horrendous cold and is deathly afraid Elizabeth will contract it."

"How considerate of her. Not many young ladies think beyond themselves at her age."

Darcy smiled. "Not many young ladies are my sister."

"You and your cousin, Colonel Fitzwilliam, have done an admirable job of raising her. I know Maxwell speaks quite highly of her, given her age."

"He does?" Darcy's interest moved to Max, his eyes narrowing as he shifted into elder brother mode. "And does he speak of my sister often?"

"Stand down, Darcy." He slapped Darcy on the shoulder. "My family has known your family for generations. I am sure he looks upon her as a younger cousin. He speaks of her as often as he speaks of you. There. Satisfied?"

"Moderately." A soft smile graced his face as Elizabeth approached the two of them. "My wife. Have I told you how lovely you look this evening?"

"More than once, Mr. Darcy." Elizabeth's eyes sparkled. "How are you, Lord George? It is my understanding you may be taking over your mother's estate in Cambridgeshire?"

"How on earth did you know that?" George asked. "I signed the papers with Mother's solicitors just this past week."

"I have my sources, Lord George and if you think I am going to give them up without some incentives, you are mistaken."

George couldn't help himself, he burst out laughing. "What kind of incentives are we speaking of, dare I ask?"

Elizabeth leaned across Darcy's body and whispered, as though imparting a great secret. "Your brother's cook's recipe for scones. Lately, I crave the taste of them most ardently and our cook cannot figure out what missing ingredient makes yours so different."

"So, for a melt-in-your-mouth scone, you will give up your source?"

"Sadly, yes." Elizabeth shrugged her shoulders with a simple elegance. "I would never make a good spy."

"Thank goodness for that." Darcy murmured and lifted her gloved hand to his lips. "I could not bear to lose the two of you."

While Elizabeth smiled and flushed again at her husband's tone, George's interest was captured by Darcy's phrase, 'the two of you'. He slid his glance lower and noticed an almost imperceptible roundness beneath Mrs. Darcy's gown. George rocked back on his heels and understood now why Mr. Darcy was content. He was a happily situated man, indeed.

The dinner bell sounded and Max's butler appeared in the doorway.

"Dinner is served, Your Grace."

As Miss Mary Bennet was the eldest single woman, Max offered her his arm and George happily escorted Miss Catherine into the dining room, suddenly glad Darcy left his younger sister at home with her tutors for this trip.

"Miss Catherine, I return to Cambridgeshire at the end of this week. Might I deliver your father's book for you?"

"How thoughtful of you, Lord George, but rarely do I see surprise in my father's eyes and I do not want to miss out on the occasion."

"Of course, I also would not want to deprive you of that pleasure."

Confound it, he'd have to obtain the book by other means.

Catherine was seated across and down the table from him, so he was unable to enjoy a semi-private tête-à-tête with her. As such, he turned his attention to his future sister, Miss Caroline Bingley, who regaled him with candid observations about his youngest brother. He was delighted in the knowledge that she challenged him. Nathan needed a partner in life, not a docile doormat.

After the gentleman had spent some time with their port, they joined the ladies in the drawing room. Mary was quietly playing the pianoforte and the rest of the ladies were gathered together, deep in pleasant conversation. When the men entered, Max asked them all if they would like to play a word game called Consequence. Everyone agreed and quickly arranged the chairs so they were placed in a circular fashion around the room.

Max quickly explained the rules and wrote down on a single sheet the instructions.

"As your host, I shall begin the game and pass the sheet of paper to my right, which means you, Darcy will be second, followed by Elizabeth, etc., etc. Now, this sheet" – he held up the document with the writing prompts – "will be passed along with the blank sheet so that you do not forget what you are to write next. Does everyone understand the game?"

At their nods, Max scribbled a word on the paper and folded the sheet just enough to cover his answer yet leaving the document available for the next person to write on. Darcy took some time to look over the second sheet with the writing prompts.

Adjective for a gentleman

Gentleman's name

MET:

Adjective for a lady

Lady's name

AT:

Where they met

What he wore

What she wore

He said to her

She said to him

The consequence was

What the world said

Once the document reached Nathan, who was last to participate, Max took the sheet from him and handed it to Caroline.

"Caroline, seeing as you did not have the chance to write down something, would you do the honor of reading?"

"I would love to." Caroline scanned the page quickly, her full lips lifting into a smile as she reached the end. She then looked around the room and began reading.

"Clever Mr. Darcy **MET** Defiant Mrs. Jane Bingley **AT** The George Inn. He wore mud-spattered boots. She wore a diamond tiara. He said to her, Have you any porridge? She said to him, I believe we are going to have rain. The consequence was they imbibed in too much wine. The world said, My Kingdom for a horse!"

They all laughed gaily and Darcy declared, "I know Charles wrote 'have you any porridge?' as he is always thinking of his next meal. You shall have to watch him, Jane. He will blossom into a 'well-rounded' gentleman if you give him free rein over the table."

Jane smiled and blushed before replying. "Between his textile mills to the north and his shipping concerns in Liverpool, Charles does not have time to indulge as he once did."

"My Angel, always looking out for me." Bingley bestowed yet another loving glance upon his serene wife.

"Would you all like to play another round?" Max asked. At their affirmative, he picked up another piece of paper and handed it, along with a pencil, to Caroline. "Your turn to go first, and this time we shall pass to the left."

Caroline tapped the pencil against her lip before a spark of mischief sparkled in her eyes. She quickly scribbled a word, folded the paper and handed it to Nathan. From there it passed to Mr. Gardiner, to Mrs. Gardiner, to Bingley, to Mrs. Bingley, to Miss Bennet, then himself, Catherine, Elizabeth, ending with Darcy, who handed the finished document to Max.

With a smile, Max unfolded the document completely, perused their scribblings and almost laughed out loud. Impatiently they waited as he cleared his throat and began.

Impetuous Lord George Kerr MET genteel Miss Catherine Bennet AT Netherfield Park. He wore a swirling black cape. She wore a festive hat adorned with feathers. He said to her, "Get thee to a nunnery!" She said to him, "All that glisters is not gold." The consequence was: they discovered a dread secret. The world said, "God moves in a mysterious way, His wonders to perform."

"I love Cowper," Elizabeth enthused. "You are so brilliant, Mr. Darcy."

"I see that my brother and Miss Catherine stole from the bard, although I am surprised George remembers any lines as he has a tendency to fall asleep during most performances." Max teased while putting away the paper and pencil into a basket the footman had provided.

"Not fair, brother. I do not fall asleep, I merely close my eyes to avoid any and all distractions, so that I may concentrate on the talented thespians who grace the stage."

Both Darcy and Max laughed out loud at his protest.

"Nay, George. I have heard a gentle snore emit from you on more than one occasion," Darcy teased, "but I will give you credit for having knowledge of his plays, at least in the written form."

"You wound me, Darcy. Now the ladies will think I am a slothful cad and never wish to attend the theater with me, no matter how hard I beg."

"I wonder what dread secret they discovered," Caroline mused. "That was very clever of you, Elizabeth."

"I pictured them in some dark castle, one from King Henry VIII's time, and they stumble upon a secret door, which led to a secret room, where they found a secret box–"

"Lizzy! How many secrets were we going to uncover in this imaginative world?" Catherine cried out. That she'd enjoyed the game was evident by the lovely smile that complimented her bright eyes.

"Oh, not long. Only until we found the body of a long-forgotten nobleman, who died hiding from marauding Vikings."

"That is preposterous," Miss Bennet said. "King Henry's castles were built long after the Vikings raided our country."

"You are quite right, Mary. Oh dear," Lizzy shrugged, showing not one stitch of remorse. "I guess then we shall have to say they found a secret niche where scandalous papers were stashed. Documents that threatened the very life of our King."

George gave a start at how close Elizabeth came to what had actually happened during his trip to Cambridgeshire. If he wasn't absolutely positive that she was *not* a spy, and that until a few days ago had been safely ensconced in Pemberley, he'd have sworn she knew his secret.

"Lizzy, you should take pen to paper and write down these fantastical notions. You have the beginnings of a great adventure," Mrs. Gardiner said in a cheerful voice.

Elizabeth's family all nodded in agreement, and Darcy looked upon his wife with an indulgent, happy smile.

"That's my Elizabeth. Always the adventurer."

"I wasn't aware you enjoyed the bard this much. I believe this is the second time you have quoted from his works," George said in a sotto voice to Catherine.

"When you live in the country and there are many days and nights of inclement weather, five girls will do almost anything to pass the time." She let her gaze roam over her three sisters in attendance. "I myself once played Mercutio in Romeo and

Juliet. I also was the apothecary and Juliet's mother. With only five, you had to take on multiple roles," she explained. "We had a much more rounded cast when the Lucas sisters joined in."

"Dare I assume who held the lead roles?" George thought for sure the two eldest Bennet sisters would have commandeered the roles of Romeo and Juliet.

"You can guess, but I do not think you would be correct," she teased and laughed at his raised brow. "Lydia begged to play Romeo, as she wanted to fight a duel with swords, and Jane played Juliet, although she refused to let Lydia pretend kiss her."

"You must have had a merry time of it."

"We did. Mama and Papa watched the whole thing and I think it is the only time I ever saw them laugh so much, especially when Jane pretended a red scarf was blood spurting from her bosom after she struck the fatal blow with her dagger."

The image of the man he'd killed at Evangeline's flooded his memory. What would Miss Catherine say if he told her, in no uncertain terms, that blood didn't spurt from a mortal chest wound. Rather it spread with a slow finality across their chest.

"George, are you all right?" Nathan asked. "You look like you have seen a ghost."

He snapped out of the memory and quickly smiled.

"No ghosts, just thinking about secret rooms. I wonder how many old castles have them."

The conversation veered to the great houses of England and tales of ancient kings and queens and George breathed a sigh of relief. He hoped Catherine hadn't thought his behavior rude. The evening had been almost perfect, the exception being that he didn't get to spend enough time in conversation with her.

Later that night, after their guests departed, he enjoyed a glass of port with his brothers in the study. Rarely were all three of them in the same house, let alone the same room.

"It is good to see you, Nathan. I have recently been told that letters just are not the same as hearing your voice, and I concur."

"You sound positively maudlin, George. Are you becoming soft in your old age?"

"Laugh, if you must. I spent too many nights worrying about you in France to feel shame at my affection for you - misplaced as it is."

Max and Nathan both laughed out loud.

"I survived France and hope this continuing conflict resolves itself soon. Too many good men are dying, on both sides," Nathan said.

Silently George agreed with him. In France he'd seen the ravages of war, the stark inhumanity on a daily basis. Dark memories threatened to invade his thoughts, only to be waylaid by Max's next statement.

"You are escorting Caroline and the other ladies to Gunter's tomorrow?"

"Yes," Nathan replied, a self-satisfied smile curving his lips. "I would rather have my fiancé alone for the afternoon, but given that we are not yet out of half-mourning, I will take whatever small pleasures which present themselves."

"Might I join you, brother?" George placed his cut glass on a side table. "I may provide a small diversion with the other ladies, if you so desire."

CATHERINE

Nathan's affirmative gave him leave to breathe again. During dinner, the solution to the acquisition of Mr. Bennet's book had presented itself in a most ingenious way. It was so simple it was laughable, but then, as he'd discovered many times, the best solutions usually were quite simplistic in nature. Now all he had to do was maneuver the surprisingly stubborn Miss Catherine Bennet into giving him possession of the book for one afternoon.

Chapter Twelve

Rising several hours prior to the group's trip to Gunter's, George quickly penned a note to Catherine asking that she bring along the book. He promised to enlighten her to the reason when he arrived with Nathan. He then broke his fast and called for the carriage.

"Take me to Hatchard's," George instructed Henry.

"Yes, sir."

With that Henry skillfully maneuvered them through the busy streets and George was soon deposited directly in front of the popular bookstore. In a little over half an hour he was on his way to Darcy's town house, a discreetly wrapped package hidden beneath the squabs of his carriage.

The night previous, it had been agreed upon by all parties involved that Nathan would transport Caroline and Jane Bingley, and George would escort Elizabeth Darcy, Miss Bennet and Catherine. He hoped, no, he prayed fervently Catherine would agree with his request and bring the book with her.

He alighted from the carriage and approached the entrance to Darcy House. The heavy mahogany door was opened by the butler.

"Good afternoon, Hutchins," he said by way of greeting the elderly man.

"Good afternoon, Lord Kerr. Mrs. Darcy, your brother and the other ladies await you in the yellow parlor."

A footman took his hat and gloves and he followed the austere butler to a pleasant room situated on the left side of the massive entrance way. He was as familiar with this house as he was his own. He, Maxwell, Nathan and Darcy had spent many school vacations in both homes along with Darcy's cousin, Colonel Fitzwilliam.

His gaze followed lines of the shining mahogany balustrade that curved up to the second floor. How many times had they all slid down its smooth surface. Before his father died, young Fitzwilliam Darcy had a touch of mischief in him and was game for all sorts of foolish boyhood pranks. When the elder Mr. Darcy passed, he assumed the heavy mantle of everything Pemberley and George often wondered if he'd ever see the lighthearted man he knew and loved as a brother.

However, after seeing him with his vivacious bride, he worried no more. Happiness shone through Darcy's eyes and his ready laugh assured him that Elizabeth Darcy, nee Bennet, was the best thing that happened in his life. There was something about the Bennet ladies that made men want to cherish them, evidenced by the absolutely besotted glances he caught between Charles and Jane. Even Caroline, who was very much in love with his brother, commented on how disgustingly sweet they were together.

"I shall have to eat stale crackers for a month after being in their company. One can stomach only so much sugar in a day," she'd declared near the end of their dinner the other night.

He'd laughed at her observation, not wanting to point out that she and Nathan were as bad, if not worse than Mr. and Mrs. Charles Bingley.

Upon entering the parlor, he noted Miss Bennet and Catherine seated on a small couch across from Mrs. Bingley and Mrs. Darcy, while Nathan and Caroline occupied another small settee closer to the window. Miss Bennet looked surprisingly bright this morning and it took George a few minutes to realize that she was attired in a light green muslin dress, eschewing the dove greys and browns which had been a staple of her wardrobe for as long as he'd known her. It seemed this visit to London was slowly changing the more somber Bennet sister. For that he was glad. He'd come to appreciate the dry wit and intelligence she only showed amongst those she felt comfortable.

But it was Miss Catherine who stole his breath. The cream dress and cranberry spencer she wore was a perfect foil for her dark coloring. It was only when Nathan cleared his throat loudly did George realize he was staring.

"Excuse me for staring." He decided to address his faux pas head on. "I'm in awe of all the beauty surrounding me this morning. In fact, I'm quite jealous of Nathan that he has had the pleasure of your company longer than I."

"Lord George, you should temper your admiration," Caroline said with a small trill of laughter. "I might toss aside your brother and attach myself to you."

Nathan gave George a dark look before taking his betrothed's hand in his. He brought her fingers to his lips and murmured against them, "You are completely mad and headed for Bedlam if you entertain the notion for even one minute that I would let you go."

George realized a person would have to be blind not to see how much Caroline was touched by his brother's possessive remark. She leaned toward Nathan and five pairs of eyes waited to see if they would kiss. When Nathan quirked his eyebrow, she stopped and blushed.

"I believe that is our cue to take our leave or the day will get away from us." Elizabeth stood and began ushering all of them toward the vestibule. After all the ladies had passed by him, George bumped Nathan with his shoulder.

"Nice recovery, little brother."

"Be grateful for Caroline's quick wit, otherwise everyone would know how much you care for a certain young miss from Hertfordshire."

Nathan's words stayed with George as he made his way outside. Did everyone see how much he admired Miss Catherine Bennet? Before entering the carriage, Catherine handed him the book, still wrapped in its brown paper packaging.

"You have my curiosity, Lord George. I spent most of the morning wondering what surprise you have in store for me today."

"I believe you will like it." He directed his attention toward Elizabeth. "Mrs. Darcy, do you mind if we attend Hatchard's before proceeding to Gunter's. I have a proposition with regard to the book Miss Catherine purchased for your father."

"I have no objection. Is Lord Nathan aware we will be delayed?"

"Yes, I told him we would be about fifteen minutes and he was agreeable."

"I am sure he was," came Mrs. Darcy's dry reply.

With only Mrs. Jane Bingley as a chaperone, Nathan and Caroline would have plenty of time to hold hands and have quiet words. George helped the ladies into the carriage and then joined them, sitting atop the hidden book he'd previously purchased and carefully wedged Catherine's book between the seat and inside panel of the carriage.

Within minutes, their carriage drew to a stop in front of the book store. As he moved to exit, he pretended to bump Catherine's package onto the floor.

"How clumsy of me," he muttered loud enough for the ladies to hear.

He then reached beneath the seat and pulled out his package, grateful for the natural dimness within an enclosed carriage. After alighting, he assisted all the ladies to the pavement. With a nod to Henry, he then turned and followed the ladies into Hatchard's assured that his driver would retrieve the book and store it safely in the lock box beneath his seat.

For the first time in weeks, ever since she'd gained possession of such a potential threat, not only to England but to herself, George felt a great weight roll off his shoulders. Now he could focus his attention solely on Miss Catherine Bennet of Longbourn.

"YOU WISH TO HAVE A book plate with Papa's name and estate placed inside the book?"

Kitty was flabbergasted. Never in her craziest of dreams would she think of doing something so extravagant. Lord George's eyes flashed with delight at having surprised her.

"I do. Not everyone has a first edition of such a popular novel and this paves the way for other treasures to be added, making his library a little more prestigious."

"Although a thoughtful gift, Lord George, I do not have the funds for such fripperies."

His brow furrowed and for a moment she thought she saw a trace of frustration flit across his handsome face. It disappeared as fast as it arrived and he smiled, again.

"I have told you more than once of how dreadful I feel at having almost run you over and this small token will almost pay my debt of gratitude."

"Almost?" she queried. What more could he do? He'd exceeded any and all expectations she'd never had.

"Yes, almost. I have something else I would like to discuss with you later today."

"Very well," she sighed out, not willing to continue to argue in front of her sisters. "I agree to a book plate for Papa."

"Excellent, Miss Catherine. Come this way."

She and Lord George made their way to the back of the store while Lizzy and Mary browsed the shelves. Soon they were at a small counter and were greeted by a middle-aged man. George unwrapped the book and handed the copy of *Robinson Caruso* to the clerk. Catherine then provided the clerk with her father's name and correct spelling of Longbourn. They were assured the book would be ready within the hour and all four of them left to meet up with Nathan, Caroline and Jane.

"MISS CATHERINE, BEFORE we return for your father's book, would you take a stroll with me in the park?"

174

They'd finished enjoying their iced drinks and the ladies were discussing which shops to attend next. Caroline expressed a great desire to visit a prominent milliner a few shops down the street.

Why would Lord George wish to walk with her, alone? Aware of the speculative glances everyone sent their way, she felt a touch of panic.

"I will, if Mary joins us." She knew Mary didn't share the same passion as her other sisters for bonnets and ribbons and would make a pleasant chaperone.

Mary nodded her assent and with that George made plans with Nathan to meet them all at Hatchard's in an hour. They crossed the street and began walking down the path lined with flowering bushes which led to a small fountain and a few benches scattered at intervals.

Their pace was moderate, as her ankle remained weak and she couldn't proceed at her normal speed. When they reached the fountain, Mary asked if she could rest for a moment and peruse the book she'd purchased while they were at Hatchard's.

"Of course, Mary. Lord George and I will stay within sight and stroll around the fountain."

Mary gave her a small smile and settled on the bench. Lord George extended his arm and Catherine carefully laid her fingers atop his forearm. He placed his hand over her fingers and drew her closer.

"I do not want you falling and re-injuring yourself, otherwise I might have to buy a whole library full of books for your father."

Almost against her will, she laughed. Only Lord George knew how to make light of her nervousness.

"Very well, although if Papa were here, he might encourage you to toss me in the fountain so that he could build a new wing to house all his books."

"Ha," Lord George laughed out loud. "You have a surprisingly quick wit, Miss Catherine."

"Thank you," she replied.

They'd proceeded to the other side of the fountain when she felt Lord George's arm tense. There was no one near, nor was anyone walking toward them so she wondered why he exhibited such a strange nervousness.

"Miss Catherine. I was going to wait until we knew one another a little better before I... before we...," he seemed to flounder for words. "I would like permission to speak with your father."

"About what?" she asked in surprise.

For what reason could he wish to speak with Papa? Did he wish to query further about compensation for her injuries? Lord George interrupted her internal musings and turned to face her, taking possession of both her hands.

"I wish to seek his permission to court you."

WITH A GASP, SHE TURNED to face him, her eyes wide. Momentarily distracted by the look of abject fear in her eyes, he nearly missed her soft reply.

"You wish to... court me."

He briefly registered she said it as a statement, not as a question.

"Yes, I wish to court you – most ardently."

"But... but, you hardly know me."

"Ever since last November at Pemberley you have been my silent companion. My greatest fear was that someone else would capture your heart before I had a chance to see you again."

"I will never marry." She pulled her hands from his and turned away.

The world dropped from beneath his feet and he felt as though he were falling a great distance. He blurted out 'Why not?' before he could stop himself. He admitted she had surprised him with her response. Wasn't marriage the goal of all young ladies?

"You wouldn't understand."

"Miss Catherine." He longed to take her hand in his again and satisfied his need to touch her with taking her arm and turning her to face him. "Please explain. I promise I won't be angry."

Her indecision displayed itself by the way she nibbled one corner of her bottom lip and he sorely wished to stop her with a kiss. He schooled his features to show only patience, not passion.

"I...Well..." He watched as she seemed to struggled to find words. "I don't want a marriage like Mama and Papa."

This? This is what held her back? Her parents imprudent marriage? He threw caution to the wind and captured her hand, smiling slightly when she snatched it back as though burned. His beautiful, mixed up Catherine. He led them to a bench and they both sat down.

"I, for one, think your parents have a perfect marriage." He began his argument to sway her opinion.

"What?" Her startled gaze flew to his. "Surely you jest? Papa always censures Mama because she is so flighty and empty-headed. How you think that is perfect is beyond me."

"Miss Catherine," George said with a soft laugh. "Have you never watched your parents with an ambiguous eye?" At the shake of her head he continued. "Your father bellows he has the silliest of women living under his roof, but I can guarantee he would not want it any other way. And your mother, for all her fluttering and spasms, completely dotes on him. Although she may not comprehend most of what he talks about, she never interrupts and believes with all her heart he is the most educated, intelligent man in all of England."

Catherine's mouth opened slightly at this revelation of her parents and his attention was drawn to the dewy softness of her full lips. With great regret he forced himself to look away and continued to press his argument.

"Your father, on the other hand, allows your mother to be flighty and although he grumbles about how much she over-spends her pin money, has he ever refused her? She leaves him alone so he can read his beloved books in silence and he, in turn, allows her to behave in a silly manner. For them, it is the perfect match."

"But, Mama can at times be so vulgar. She embarrasses us constantly with talk of meeting rich gentleman–" She stopped midsentence. "Forgive me, Lord George. Mama forgets at times that more elevated people do not go around talking about how much wealth a person possesses."

"That is where you are wrong," he said with a derisive laugh. "While your mother has some crude tendencies – nothing that alarms me to the point of cutting all contact with your family," he soothed when her eyes flashed with annoyance, "However, I can assure you with absolute certainty your mother is a soft bellied fish compared to the barracudas which swim amongst London's first circles."

"Oh my. This sounds like you have had some bitter encounters."

He sighed, troubled that he'd vented some of his loathing of London's society in her direction.

"I would take your witty father and your flighty mother any day of the week. They at least reside together in their home and share conversation, regardless of how silly it might sound."

"I never thought of it that way," she said softly. "How right you are."

"Of course, I am right. Just as I am right you shall marry." He shifted closer, inhaling her sweet scent of lavender. "Maybe even to me."

"Fair warning, Lord Kerr. I am not my mother." She refused to meet his gaze and fussed with the button on her glove. "I will not dote on any man, nor do I think you are the most educated man in all of England."

"But you think I am intelligent, yes?"

She nodded, her cheeks blooming a delicate shade of pink as she turned her face to look back at Miss Bennet, exposing the elegant line of her neck. He longed to lift his hand and tuck the errant curl forever escaping her bonnet behind her ear.

He smiled, feeling a spurt of satisfaction. She hadn't repeated her statement of never marrying when he'd put forward his cheeky suggestion. Was that not proof enough she at least thought about him? Maybe even dallied in a few day dreams?

"Catherine?" he whispered, half in anguish, half in hope. "With your permission, I would like to ride to Longbourn and speak with your father and after a few months, ask for your hand in marriage."

She stayed silent for so long, he wondered if she'd heard his desperate plea.

"No," she finally answered.

"Pardon?" Surely, she hadn't denied his request again.

For a brief moment her shoulders drooped and curved slightly in, as though protecting herself from some unknown force. If he knew anything about body language, what he witnessed assured him she was experiencing deep remorse, or worse, a sense of loss. After an agonizing few seconds of silence, she stood and faced him. "I thank you for the honor you have bestowed on me, but I cannot accept knowing that in the end I would refuse any offer of marriage."

Before he could utter another word, she turned around and walked as best she could with an injured ankle toward Miss Bennet. All coherent thought fled from his mind and as such, he remained seated on the bench.

Why would she refuse him?

Then, it hit him. She must have heard rumors of his reputation as a debauched rake. Not for the first time he cursed the fact he'd played the part of a rogue in order to hide his clandestine operation with Evangeline. He wanted to go home and lick his wounds, but as a gentleman he had to escort the two Miss Bennet's back to their sister's home. Besides, chasing after Catherine wouldn't make her listen. Words were empty, they meant nothing without action. He would have to 'show' he was a changed man and how much he loved her.

He caught up with her before she'd even gone a few yards. "Miss Catherine," he called softly.

She continued on as though he hadn't spoken. He came abreast and then angled his body in her direct path so that she'd have to either slow down or stop. She came to a full stop, but kept her head lowered, the wide brim of her bonnet obscuring his view of her face.

"Miss Catherine, I beg your forgiveness. Please allow me to escort you back to your sister. I will not speak another word on this topic." At least for today, he promised himself.

After what seemed like an eternity, she placed her fingers on his extended arm and they continued at a slower pace toward Miss Bennet, who's interest remained absorbed by her book. He gave silent thanks for the single-minded focus she had when it came to reading. Much the same as she'd displayed at Longbourn after Catherine's accident.

For Catherine's sake, he was glad Miss Bennet hadn't witnessed their somewhat private exchange. Catherine may choose to share what happened with her sister and there was nothing he could do about it. However, her revelation might be a good idea as Miss Bennet, a practical sort of girl, might counsel Catherine to reconsider his offer.

When they were still a dozen yards away from Miss Bennet, Catherine fumbled to open her reticule. He risked peeking beneath the brim of her bonnet and saw a glistening trail of tears streaking down her pale cheeks. Without thought, he reached into his pocket and provided her with one of his own monogrammed linen handkerchiefs.

"Thank you," she murmured.

"You are welcome," he whispered back. "Would you like to watch the ducks for a brief moment before we return to Miss Bennet?"

He wished to provide her with some much-needed time in order to compose herself before they reached her sister. He was rewarded with a quick glance from under her bonnet and a tremulous smile.

"Thank you, Lord George. After my abominable behavior, you still show me such kindness."

"I would present you with the sun and moon, if possible. Giving you a moment of peace is the least I could do."

Chapter Thirteen

Tears flowed freely down Kitty's cheeks, soaking her pillow. At first her heart soared at the thought of Lord George courting her with the purpose of marriage, then reality shoved its way into her brain and reminded her that on their wedding night he'd discover her deepest, darkest secret.

Not for the first time she railed against the fact she could never marry. Yes, Papa told her not to refuse a good gentleman and she knew he'd meant Lord George, but how could she in good conscience marry him without telling him about her past? Once he knew all the sordid details, he'd cut her direct and at least this way she had a small chance of maintaining a friendship.

When he'd leaned in and she thought he might kiss her, she fought to keep a clear head. Her brain ran around like a silly goose thinking of reasonable ways to refuse him when she'd remembered one small comment made by Mrs. Hurst when the ladies had tea last week.

She'd mused about how tame Lord George's behavior had been these past few months. According to the ladies she gossiped with, he had quite the reputation of being a favorite of the Countess of Anstruther, whose husband was conveniently over on the Continent. At the time, Kitty disregarded her catty observations as when Lord George and the Countess spoke at Gunter's, she'd not noticed one iota of attraction between them, only a tense nervousness on both their parts.

In fact, their nervousness began when she recognized Lady Harriet. Deep in her gut, she knew something beyond her reasoning capabilities was going on between these two supposed friends, and it was not a lover's tiff. Lord George had gone as still as a cat, waiting for its prey to make a wrong move, and the Countess had been quite flustered at her calling out to Lady Harriet although she'd carried on the rest of her visit with aplomb.

Not for one minute did Kitty buy her explanation the young girl was her companion, Miss Bledsoe. The scar which marred Lady Harriet's top lip was distinctive in shape. She should know. She was there when Lady Harriet received it at the hand of her father, Viscount Stanhope.

"Kitty?"

A soft knock at the door accompanied Mary's call.

"Come in, Mary." She hurried to straighten her dress and with shaky hands, patted her hair in place.

Her elder sister opened the door, took one look at her redrimmed eyes, sat on the edge of the bed and wrapped her in a hug. After a few minutes they parted and Mary tilted her head and gave her a warm, if quizzical look.

"I wondered what happened at the park today. Has Lord George told you he is withdrawing his attention?"

Fresh tears threatened to spurt and flow again. Kitty fought to keep them at bay as she answered.

"No, quite the opposite in fact."

"Then why are you crying your eyes out?"

"I refused him."

"You what?" Mary stood and stared at her, an incredulous look replacing the earlier affectionate one. "He is absolutely besotted with you and willing to overlook our low society."

"I know, but I cannot marry him." She fumbled for the linen handkerchief Lord George provided earlier in the day and dabbed at her eyes.

Mary sat back on the bed. "Does it have something to do with this burden you refuse to let go?"

Kitty longed to share that burden but couldn't stand the thought of her sister thinking ill of her. Not after she'd tried so hard this year to behave in a more ladylike manner. Everyone had been disgusted by Lydia's behavior with Wickham, what would they do if they knew her truth?

She rose to her feet and paced to the window. Her room overlooked the park across the street. Lizzy and Darcy had a lovely home in Mayfair and she once again felt such a surge of gratitude for her new brother. He loved her sister to distraction and in turn, showed favor to Lizzy's silly family. All that would cease for her if she told her secret.

"Yes, in some way it does," she finally answered Mary's question. "But he also has the reputation of being a dangerous libertine. I liked his friendship but cannot trust that his affection would remain true to me and me alone. My heart would break if we married and he broke our vows."

She felt a pinch of regret at throwing most of the blame at Lord George's feet. Yes, she'd heard rumors but, in all truthfulness, she didn't give them much credit. His behavior had been of a true gentleman and there was an inherent honesty about

him, something intangible. She couldn't break his heart in order to pacify hers.

Mary sat in silence and Kitty rejoined her on the bed. After
a few minutes, Mary clasped their hands together. When she
bowed her head, Kitty followed suit.

"Heavenly Father, You alone know the obstacles Catherine
faces. I pray You provide her with peace. The peace You
promised that passes all understanding. Make straight her
crooked path and continue to hold her in the palm of Your
hand. Amen."

Kitty murmured 'amen' with Mary and they sat in this attitude for a few more minutes.

"Thank you, Mary. Your prayer means so much to me."

Mary cupped her face and held her gaze for what seemed
like eternity.

"Catherine. Do not forget you can enter His court anytime
in prayer. You do not need me to hold your hand anymore."

With that she rose to her feet and with a reminder that dinner would be soon, exited.

Kitty twisted the handkerchief with her fingers and
thought of Lord George's final words before they returned to
Mary. *I would present you with the sun and moon, if possible.
Giving you a moment of peace is the least I could do.* She'd known
he liked her but never once thought he'd wish to court her so
soon after their meeting again. However, he also said she'd been
his silent companion since Lizzy's wedding, which meant he'd
held some sort of tendré for her these past six months.

She let out a soft whoosh of air as his words began to per-
meate her heart. Did he truly love her and this was not a passing fancy? Hope gave way to anguish. She couldn't lead him on.

Far better to break his heart now than later. She was reminded of Hill's remedy whenever they'd had a bad cut and the dressing needed to be changed. Better to rip the binding off in one quick move than fold it back one painful inch at a time. She needed to rip the binding off his heart and let him dress it with something new and clean, which she was not.

With that she proceeded to wash her face and fix her hair before attending dinner. Her demeanor was calm and her lips held a smile, even though her heart continued to break. She would survive. She would continue on. She'd done this before; she could do it again.

SHE'D REFUSED HIM. She'd refused him. Like a never-ending loop the thought continued to taunt him. He knew she cared for him. He'd been around enough women to know when a lady was receptive to his advances, and if the soft blushes and the dilation of her pupils whenever he came near were not enough of an indicator, the involuntary parting of her lips spoke of her attraction in ways words couldn't. Then why had she refused him? Nothing made sense other than she had to have heard of his reputation. What else would keep her from accepting a courtship?

In a perverse way he was proud of the fact she'd stand strong on these principals. When he finally won her heart, he knew she'd be a faithful companion. All his life he'd looked for someone who would complement him the way his mother complemented his father. They had a marriage based on love, which was a rarity amongst the *ton*, and he wanted nothing less for himself.

Many nights, when their parents thought the boys were safe in their beds, he'd sneak down and watch them. It was not unusual to find their mother curled up against their father as they cuddled before a toasty fire speaking in low tones, or for them to dance to unheard music in the enormous ballroom.

He desired the same with Catherine and nothing would stand in his way. Unfortunately, he didn't take into account the stubbornness of one Miss Catherine Bennet of Longbourn. For three weeks he'd left his card with no response. He visited Darcy, as per usual, but the ladies were always out doing their own social calls and when he accepted an invite to dinner at Darcy house, only Darcy and his wife greeted him at the door as Catherine and Miss Bennet had accepted their own invitation to dine at the Bingley's.

This pattern repeated itself for another month until Darcy and his family removed to Pemberley for Elizabeth's confinement. Never before had he been so frustrated with no place to vent. His brother Maxwell finally cornered him in the library, nursing his third, fourth, maybe even fifth snifter of brandy. Mayhap it was his eighth.

"George, you must stop this destructive behavior. What has come over you?"

"Why?"

Max, framed in the door of the library, openly gaped at his belligerent response. He then proceeded into the room, plucked the snifter out of George's hand and placed it on a table far from George's reach.

"Never before have I seen you behave in such a deplorable manner, and as you have crafted a fine reputation these past few years, this is saying something. You prowl around the house growling at the servants, you were short with Mother the other night, and you attend White's looking to start a fight with anyone who happens to glance your way." Max placed his hands on his hips and glared down at him. "What do you have to say for yourself."

The words of his elder brother rained down on him and he acknowledged everything Max said was true. The sad fact was, he wasn't sorry for his behavior. For years the *ton* and his family labeled him as a rogue and because of that deplorable nomenclature, he'd lost the woman he loved. Why not embrace the persona he'd created and drown his sorrows? She'd refused him. She'd cut him out of her life in a most decisive manner.

"I say don't glance my way if you think I am edging for a fight."

"George," Maxwell sighed out. "This is not *you*. I know everyone thinks you wild, but I am firm in my belief that you are not. I may have leaned that way until you told me, in no uncertain terms, you would stand before the Lord with a clean heart. You meant those words and I realized that for some reason known only to you, you were putting on a façade. Please tell me what has brought you so low."

For the first time in years, George felt tears welling in his eyes. He hadn't cried since he was a school boy, but Max's words poked at his heart and brought his suffering to the top.

"She refused me."

As soon as he said the words, which had been his constant companion for months, the floodgates burst and he wept openly. He didn't even notice when Max sat beside him and placed strong arms around his shoulders, patiently waiting until the tears abated.

More than a little ashamed at his outburst, he removed himself from the couch and stood in front of the fireplace.

"Forgive my outburst," he muttered, dragging the back of his hand across his eyes before turning to stare into the flames.

"No."

Astonished, he looked back at Max.

"No?"

"No." Max had the temerity to smile. "This is the first real emotion you have shown in a long, long time. Forgiveness from me is not required."

"Thank you."

"Do not thank me, little brother." Max stood as well and came to stand across from him. "Am I to understand Miss Catherine Bennet refused you?"

Pain sliced through his heart once more.

"Yes. I asked for permission to court her and she denied me. Every attempt made to see her again and talk further was cut off. She is quite determined that I not press my suit further."

"I had no idea your emotions were so engaged. I have been busy with estate business and a problematic tenant. Do you wish to fill me in on what has been going on? My limited understanding was you only met Miss Bennet—"

"Miss Catherine." George corrected automatically, savoring the flavor of her name on his tongue, painful though it was.

"You only met Miss Catherine," Max said with an elegant arch of his eyebrow at George's hasty correction, "last November at Darcy's wedding, and for some reason you have yet to share, escorted her to London and saw her here at Kerr House when they came to dinner."

"True, I first met her at Pemberley and was enamored with her from the very beginning. She was a breath of fresh air in a world of stale sameness. Although nervous at being in the company of elevated society, she did not fawn over who I was."

"It also did not hurt that she is quite beautiful."

"But that is not the only reason I sought her out. Whenever we conversed, she delighted me with her point of view. In some ways she is quite naïve and in others she sees the world for what it is. There are times when I am surprised with her assessment of a person's character. She is almost always uncannily accurate."

"All of this from so few encounters?"

George gave his brother a telling look. "Noooo...." He drew out with a longsuffering sigh. "I also escorted Miss Catherine and her sister several times shopping and enjoyed many pleasant walks in the park near their uncle's home in Cheapside. There is no other explanation other than to say she fits me. When she is by my side, all is well."

"I had no idea you were becoming so involved in this friendship. Are you sure there is no hope?"

"None. She has quit town and at this very moment is at Pemberley with her sister, Elizabeth."

"Where you shall see her at Nathan's wedding. You will have at least a week of activities in which to engage her in conversation." Max's tone became pensive. "Did Miss Catherine give you reason for her refusal?"

"Not in so many words. She thanked me for the honor and said she could not accept a courtship knowing she would refuse any offer of marriage. Naturally I assumed rumors of my reputation reached her ears and she sought to remove herself from my company."

"Think hard on her words, George. She did not refuse you, per se. She said she would refuse *any* offer of marriage. This leads me to believe she would have refused even Prinny if *he* asked."

George mulled over Max's words which resonated in his heart. Why would Catherine refuse any offer of marriage? If he discovered the reason, there was hope she might reconsider. He slapped his brother on the shoulder and turned to leave the room.

"Where are you going?" a bewildered Max called out after him.

"I only have a month to prepare," he called back.

"Prepare for what?" Max mused, but George didn't hear him. He'd already taken the stairs, two at a time and called for Pratt to prepare his bath.

For the first time since her rejection, his heart soared. In a little over four weeks he'd be at Pemberley, and so would Catherine. With the precision of Wellington, he began to plot his campaign.

Chapter Fourteen

George paced the library, the only quiet room now that Pemberley was almost stuffed to the rafters with guests. Soon it would be impossible to find any peace. The sound of a carriage approaching drew him to the window. It wasn't to see if Catherine had returned from visiting her sister Jane, he assured himself and experienced a pinch of disappointment when the door to the carriage opened and Lady Miranda Blake disembarked.

About to turn away and continue his pacing, he paused. Behind Lady Miranda was Evangeline. She accepted the hand of the footman and gave him a saucy wink, making the poor lad blush furiously, although, to give credit to the type of service Darcy expected, he never flinched or faltered in his duties.

What the deuce was she doing here? He exited the library and strode toward the front entrance. Sounds of laughter floated down the hall and when he turned the corner, Evangeline spotted him immediately.

"Lord George," she said. "What a surprise. I had hoped to see you here."

Lady Miranda laughed aloud. "My dear Countess. It is *his* brother who is marrying our dear friend, Caroline."

Evangeline waved her hand in the air. "La, I know that, Miranda. I expected to see him at dinner. I am pleasantly surprised at his greeting us."

George watched the exchange between Lady Miranda and Evangeline. How in the world had Evangeline finagled an invitation to Nathan's wedding? Through the still open door he spotted Miss Bledsoe, or rather, Lady Harriet directing the footmen to Evangeline's trunks. His perusal was interrupted by Evangeline gliding into his line of vision. He still hadn't shared with her that he was very aware of who Miss Bledsoe truly was, and she hadn't shared any details from her end, either.

They were, as his chess master would say, at a bit of a stalemate.

"Lady Miranda and I wish to wash off the dust from our travels. Would you join us for an aperitif in about fifteen minutes Lord George? I demand to know what you have been up to these past few months, and of course, I will gladly share any news worth gossiping about."

Although her tone was light and teasing, George did not miss the pointed look she flashed in his direction.

"Count me out, Evangeline," Lady Miranda said with a smile. "I have been looking forward to a non-moving rest before we dine. You will have to make do without me."

"I will see you in the drawing room, Lady Cavendish." George gave her a polite bow and walked back to the library. He passed Mr. Darcy, followed by Mrs. Reynolds who was hurrying to greet the guests and show them to their rooms.

Something was terribly wrong and he'd play along with whatever scheme Evangeline had in mind. However, knowing that she'd hid from him the true identity of Lady Harriet, he'd proceed with caution. The implicit trust he'd held for her, forged by their mutual experiences in France as they'd evaded Napoleon's men in their bid for freedom back to England, had been damaged. He knew she had a duplicitous nature, but then so did he. It was a prerequisite in order to be a successful spy.

He glanced at the clock and made his way to the drawing room, desirous of being there before she arrived. He'd watch every move she made. Listen to every nuance in her voice, perceive the shifting of her eyes. In his observations of many people, he'd noted that when they recalled something which was a true memory, they'd look to their right. If the memory or story was a lie, they'd look to their left. He wasn't sure why, but this small foible saved him more than once when dealing with a deceitful enemy. He prayed she didn't fall into the latter category.

His wait was not long and Evangeline breezed into the room, looking as though she'd just stepped out of a garden party rather than an arduous carriage ride of four hours.

"Lord George!" She moved toward him; her hands outstretched in greeting. It was only when the parlor doors closed behind her that she dropped her hands and sat on the couch. With a graceful incline of her head, she said, "Will you not join me?"

He lowered his tension filled body onto the chair across from the couch and waited. Silence reigned for only a few minutes before she shook her head slowly.

"We are at an impasse. I know you do not trust me, now that you know who Miss Bledsoe truly is." She lifted her hand to stop him from speaking. "No, say nothing. I knew the minute Miss Catherine recognized her you would begin to dig like an impatient terrier."

"You knew all the time who Reggie was, didn't you?"

"Not at first. I knew his recognizing Miss Bledsoe somehow posed a threat to her safety. If you remember, Reggie said, '*you made him very angry by running away*', and Stanhope's the only one who has been actively searching for her. I could not take the chance of him discovering her whereabouts. I do not regret my actions."

"How do you know Stanhope wasn't using her as a conduit, as a double agent?"

"If you knew how he treated his daughter..." She shuddered and closed her eyes. "MacDougal brought her to me in the dead of night over four years ago. She had been abused in a most degrading manner and would have died. Do not question how he became involved. He never volunteered and I have never asked. My home is the last place the Viscount would think to search for his errant daughter."

"This does not explain how those two men knew about our operation." From his observations, George knew she spoke the truth, but there were so many other missing pieces.

"We live in a time where friends become enemies and enemies become friends." She shrugged at his raised eyebrow. "Suffice to say, our contact in France decided their love of money outweighed their hatred of that tiny upstart. Our courier was followed every step of the way, hoping to discover the identities of the English agents, namely you and me. Once I knew Stanhope was behind the English side of the puzzle, I had my connections trace everything back to France."

"This does not explain why you are here, at Pemberley."

"It is interesting how paths cross and interconnect in the most unusual way. You received my note this past April." At his affirmative nod, she continued. "I sailed to France and had an in-depth conversation with our traitor. At first, he denied, then he bragged, and finally he pleaded. When his most tender parts were re-adjusted, he purged his soul."

George involuntarily shuddered and crossed his legs. He always knew Evangeline had a ruthless streak, evidenced with how she dealt with the traitor.

"I see you understand completely." She'd noticed his reaction and gave a knowing smile. "While there, I searched and found a cache of documents which, if found by the wrong people, would have devastatingly compromised our mission."

"Where are those documents now?"

"I have them with me."

"What?" George stood, agitated beyond endurance. "Why would you bring them here? Why not take them to the War Office?"

"Whom do I trust?" Evangeline also stood. "I do not know who *your* contact is. We've always kept these things from each other in case one of us was compromised. You are the only person I can give them to."

George strode toward the window, pushing a hand through his hair. If only Evangeline had trusted him with the identity of Lady Harriet. Maybe then all of this would have been resolved sooner. As it was, Stanhope was among the guests expected to arrive later in the day. He turned to face Evangeline.

"We have no time to waste. Stanhope will be arriving later this afternoon."

"That vile man is a guest of Mr. Darcy?"

"No, he is a guest of our family. He just happens to be staying at Pemberley. I allowed his name to remain on the list in order to keep an eye on him." He pushed a hand through his hair again. Evangeline smiled, much like a mother would with her fussy child. She came up to him and straightened his unruly locks.

"We will figure this out. Do not worry so much."

At the sound of a small gasp, George glanced over Evangeline's shoulder. Frozen in the doorway, eyes wide with hurt, stood Miss Catherine Bennet. Too late, Evangeline lowered her hand and turned to see who had captured his interest. At the sight of Lady Cavendish standing in what could only be interpreted as an intimate posture, Catherine paled. In dread fascination he watched as her shoulder's straightened and she grew a few inches taller, reminding him of a marionette being pulled up by its strings. She looked positively regal when she raised her chin, gave them both a polite nod of acknowledgement and exited the parlor.

He cursed under his breath and clenched his fingers into a fist. What must she think of him?

"Go to her." Evangeline stepped away and settled on the couch.

"I cannot," he forced through stiff lips.

"But you care for this young lady, yes?"

"We do not have an understanding. To chase after her would send the wrong message."

"And what message is that?" Evangeline arched an eyebrow at him. "A message that you love her and wish to marry?"

"Yes, I mean, no."

"No, you do not love her?"

"I do, but I cannot marry her. Not yet."

"Ahhh... I see." Evangeline toyed with the brooch at the throat of her dress. "Is it because you are secretly betrothed to someone else and must break it off? Or maybe she is being courted by some other fine young pup. There are many here this week, she will have her pick of the litter."

"Enough, Evangeline!" He dragged his hand once again through his hair. He couldn't bear the thought of another winning her heart. "Until this thing with Stanhope is finished, I dare not let him know of my regard for Miss Catherine."

"And what if Stanhope eludes us? What if he is never brought to justice, what then? Will you see her marry another, or worse, marry no one?"

KITTY HELD HER HEAD high until she reached her bed chamber. Why wouldn't Lord George rather be with a woman as beautiful as the Countess? With her exotic looks and seductive voice, she could have any man she wanted. But, why did it have to be him? She drew a deep breath and wiped the stinging tears away with the back of her hand, knowing in her heart of hearts Lord George could never be hers. She was damaged goods. Not fit to be any man's wife. He needed someone like the Countess of Anstruther.

Someone who moved within the same social circles. Someone he'd be proud to have on his arm. The Countess was titled and beautiful, an enticing combination. She, Kitty Bennet of Longbourn, had a dowry of one thousand pounds, a lackadaisical father, a mother who couldn't curb her tongue and a sister who very nearly ruined the reputation of all their sisters by her selfish actions.

Given all these wonderful attributes - she snorted in disdain - it was a miracle her two elder sisters managed to marry anyone, let alone the successful men they did. Kitty sat at the writing desk, cupped her chin in the palm of her hand and stared out the window onto the beautiful grounds of Pemberley.

The past week had been almost like a dream. At first, she'd dreaded the arrival of Lord George and his brother the Duke of Adborough. After her refusal of his proposal and then weeks of avoiding his company, she'd been almost tongue tied the first night the two brothers joined them for dinner.

But Lord George made no demands from her and was all politeness. He didn't seek to embarrass her in any way, although he most assuredly garnered the lion's share of her time whenever the gentleman joined the ladies for after dinner conversation. And during several of her rambles around the grounds of Pemberley, she'd come across him also enjoying the park. It seemed natural to walk together and have conversations that slowly became less stilted and less formal.

Then, last night, Georgiana offered to play the pianoforte so everyone could dance. When he'd approached and asked her if she'd partner with him, her heart had all but jumped out of her chest.

The shared intimacy as they moved around in time to the music was almost unbearable. Such a heady experience, having someone so handsome pay attention to her. Yet not once did Lord George hold her hand longer than polite society thought acceptable and most definitely did not importune her any further than what was necessary.

One fat tear rolled into her cupped hand, which surprised her. After all the tears she'd shed after that disastrous proposal in the park, she didn't know she could still cry. Seeing him in such an intimate manner with Lady Cavendish had torn any romantic notion of him resuming his attentions to shreds.

When she and her family returned to Longbourn she'd make plans for her future. Papa would allow her to stay at home for a few years, but once she reached the ripe old age of five and twenty, both he and Mama would wash their hands of her. Of that fact, she was sure.

This meant she had at least five years to better her mind and accomplishments. If she studied hard enough she could find employment as a lady's companion, or maybe as a governess. She had a modest knowledge of French and surely in five years she could conquer Latin. When she embarked on her career, she'd be well armed and well informed. Darcy would know of reputable families looking for a gentlewoman to guide their children, or of an aging mother in need of a grateful companion.

With a feasible plan in action settled in her mind, Kitty dried her tears and washed her face. No more crying over things that could never be. She'd known this for over ten years and it was time to act like a woman, not a child. Her attention was caught by a flash of blue between the trees lining the garden, the same blue as the jacket Lord George was wearing.

She leaned closer to the window and watched the man break free of the trees. Yes, it was him and he was headed to the stables. Her heart constricted at the sight of his lithe body, moving with athletic grace. He was everything she'd ever hoped for. Everything she'd ever wanted and couldn't have.

The tears fell once again and this time she didn't stop them.

Chapter Fifteen

I *must speak with you, most urgently.*
   Meet me in the library
   E.C.

George read the missive again and tucked it inside the book he was reading, noting with irony he was already at the suggested rendezvous site. There was no time to meet with Evangeline. Stanhope's carriage was but an hour away. George's man had arrived only a few minutes ago ahead of the Viscount to give him a head's up – as planned – however, Evangeline was not given over to histrionics.

He cursed softly under his breath. He'd have to risk meeting her in private and hope to high heaven Catherine did not witness what she'd assume was yet another lurid assignation. All the hard work from the past week had been torn asunder by her observing them in the drawing room. One would have to be a fool not to realize she thought they were having an affair.

He didn't have long to wait. Evangeline breezed into the room a few short minutes after one of the footmen had delivered her note. When she was assured of their privacy, she began speaking in low tones.

"We must hide Lady Harriet. If Stanhope or one of his servants see her, I cannot vouch for her safety, or worse, protect her very life."

"There will be a house full of guests. Surely he would not attempt anything with so many in attendance."

"It is not just that, Lord George. He must never find out where she has taken shelter. He may not accost her here, but once we remove to London, there is no telling when or how he will snatch her away."

"Was it really that bad?"

Evangeline narrowed her eyes and glared at him. He felt the small hairs on the back of his neck rise. Lady Cavendish rarely lost her temper and he wondered exactly what had Stanhope done to make her so protective. He didn't have to wonder any longer when she spoke these chilling words.

"Do you remember when we were fleeing for our very lives in France, the pretty young serving girl who worked at the inn near the river? The one where the soldiers stayed. The one brutalized and left for dead."

He nodded. Bile rose in his throat at the very memory of her screams and even now his hand clenched at their inhumanity and how he'd been too late to save her from their 'attentions'.

"They were but lads in leading strings compared to the way Stanhope treated his daughter." George gagged at the very thought. "He can never find Lady Harriet, for I fear for her very life."

"I shall find a place. Have her pack lightly, speed is of the essence."

He'd immediately thought of Nathan and his vicarage in Kympton. What better place for sanctuary but with a man of God in his house. He and Lady Harriet would both ride on Buttons and he needn't bother a stable hand to saddle him up as George was quite accustomed to riding bareback, if necessary. He hoped Lady Harriet was an able horsewoman. Regardless, she'd have no choice in the matter. He couldn't take the chance of anyone coming across them.

"This is one of the many things I appreciate about you. Your ability to adapt to any situation. More than once you saved our lives in France. Thinking on your feet is your strength."

"Have *Miss Bledsoe* meet me in the stables after dinner. The moon is near full and there will be enough light I can escort her to a place of safety."

"You already know where you are taking her? Without consulting anyone?"

"I do, and the less you know, the less you can reveal if pressed."

Evangeline rested her hand on his arm and squeezed.

"Thank you, my friend. I owe you a debt of gratitude that can never be repaid."

"Think nothing of it. Now, I must go. Stanhope arrives within the hour and I wish to be on hand when he arrives. I need to see who accompanies him so that I may watch their activities."

"Do not be afraid to use me in this endeavor. I do not believe Stanhope knows of my involvement and I can be a second set of eyes in a crowd of people."

"Thank you, Lady Cavendish. I bid you good day."

He gave her a polite bow and exited the room, heaving a sigh of relief at no one witnessing him exit the library.

KITTY FOLLOWED MARY into the drawing room, astonished by how many guests were already encamped about the room prior to dinner. With relief she noted Mr. Darcy's tall form near the French doors which led out to a terraced patio and the two sisters began to weave their way across the room. Beside Darcy stood Lizzy, Charles and Jane, along with Nathan and Caroline. To say that Caroline glowed with happiness would have been a colossal understatement. It was like saying the sun was a smidgeon too bright to look upon directly.

Kitty smiled at their obvious contentment and greeted Caroline with much warmth. Such a difference from when they'd originally met in Hertfordshire.

"Caroline, Lord Nathan." She gave them both a polite curtsy. "I am so looking forward to your wedding ball tomorrow night."

Even though Caroline and Lord Nathan were not a member of Darcy's family, he'd offered them his home and his family's tradition of having a wedding ball a few days prior to the wedding so that the guests could mingle and wish the couple well. The day of the wedding was always such a hectic affair, what with the ceremony followed by the wedding breakfast, followed by the couple leaving immediately for their one-month wedding trip.

"As am I, Catherine, for it was at Darcy's wedding ball that Lord Nathan and I began an understanding of sorts."

"That we did, my love, even if it was a *mis*-understanding."

Caroline laughed gaily at the confused looks from everyone.

"Yes, it was a misunderstanding, of sorts, but I was left in no doubt how I felt about you after that incident." She blushed faintly and Kitty wondered what the incident actually was. Had Lord Nathan kissed her? The romantic side of her hoped he had, further confirmed by Lord Nathan's husky reply.

"I left with no doubt, either." His gaze lowered to her lips and Caroline, turning a delicious shade of pink, brought up her fan and flicked it back and forth, the pomander on her wrist eliciting a soothing scent of rosewater. "I love the scent of your agitation, dear Caroline, and it delights me to no end when you succumb to my teasing."

Caroline tapped him on the arm with her fan. "How you vex me, Lord Nathan."

Kitty stifled a giggle at the repetition of one of her mother's favorite saying oft heard in the Bennet household. *Oh, how you vex me, Mr. Bennet. You have no regard for my nerves.* She realized at that moment how much she missed her family, even if they were at times silly and looked forward to their arrival on the morrow.

They had an unexpected delay at one of the posting inns, with their carriage requiring a new wheel after hitting a large hole in the road. If all went well, they'd arrive a few hours before the ball.

She took the time to assess her older sisters. Lizzy had given birth to Bennet Fitzwilliam Darcy a few weeks ago and looked positively stunning in a cream over jade green dress, which complimented her matronly curves in all the right ways, if the secret smile Mr. Darcy shared with her was anything to go by.

Jane, on the other hand was nearing her confinement, and although always serenely beautiful, she tired quicker than was her wont and Kitty knew Charles would bustle her off to their rooms as soon as it was polite. It also hadn't helped that they spent the last month moving into their new estate thirty miles from Lizzy and Darcy. However, she had only a few more public functions to attend and then she could rest to her heart's content, as Charles would make sure Jane didn't lift a finger until their child was born.

Conversations ebbed and flowed around Kitty, with various guests coming up to Darcy and congratulating him on his home, wife and newborn son. In turn, they spoke with Lord Nathan and Caroline before making way for another guest to extol their good wishes.

Kitty, lulled into a sense of happiness, tensed when Lord George entered the room. As though tethered by some unseen force, his gaze captured hers within seconds. With a determined look on his face, he began to cross the room toward her.

She froze in place when her line of sight landed on the gentleman entering the room behind Lord George. She bit back a cry, pushed the back of her hand against her mouth and escaped the room as fast as humanly possible, praying she wouldn't cast up her accounts in front of Darcy's esteemed guests.

GEORGE, NEVER HAVING taken his eyes off Catherine, experienced a searing jolt of alarm when a look of abject horror crossed her face. She'd blanched whiter than a baby lamb, covered her mouth and practically ran out the terrace doors. Was she so affronted by his supposed behavior with Evangeline that she became physically ill at the sight of him?

He looked around to see if anyone else had noticed her abrupt exit and was brought up short when he heard a familiar voice murmur, "Well, well, well. The little kitty cat is here. How delightful."

He turned and noted Stanhope, a disgusting leer on his face, staring at the doors Catherine had run through. It was quite apparent the Viscount did not know he'd overheard the comment. George was well aware Catherine's family called her Kitty, although he refused to call her anything but Catherine, but how in the world did Stanhope know her? And given his experience with lurid members of the ton, the Viscount was experiencing disgusting, lecherous thoughts about her. His stomach roiled at the very idea.

He had to find her and ascertain, for his own sanity, that she was safe. With that thought in mind, he cleaved through the crowd and exited the room, catching only a glimpse of a light-colored gown moving through the trees. He tore off after her, but by the time he reached the small copse of trees, she'd disappeared. He searched for a few more minutes before turning back and re-entering the drawing room. Not wanting to draw undue attention, he approached Miss Bennet and whispered in her ear. She nodded and excused herself to family and friends and made her way out of the room.

Satisfied Miss Bennet would see to her sister, he turned his attention to Nathan and Caroline, congratulating them on their upcoming nuptials and Darcy and Elizabeth on the birth of the next Darcy heir. While pleasantly conversing, he caught the eye of Evangeline. With an almost imperceptible nod of his head, he indicated where she'd locate Stanhope.

He relaxed his vigil only slightly, knowing Evangeline would keep an eye on the disgusting piece of humanity that was Stanhope while he was engaged with family matters. His enjoyment grew when Max joined them, Miss Georgiana Darcy on his arm and Mrs. Annesley not far behind. They'd taken a turn around the glass enclosure Darcy built last year to grow vegetables all year round.

From the corner of his eye he noted a footman approach Evangeline and hand her a note. Her face paled slightly and from where he stood, he saw her hand tremble. She looked up from the missive to him directly and mouthed the word, 'Library'. Knowing she wouldn't ask him to leave such a public venue so soon after arriving, he knew what she'd received was important.

He moved around the room, stopping for light chatter with various guest and finally exited through the main doors leading to the foyer. He ascended the stairs at a sedate pace, but as soon as he reached the first landing, he sprinted down the corridor to the back staircase and from there circled around to the library. Evangeline stopped pacing as soon as he entered the room.

"What news did you receive?"

"Miss Catherine may be in grave danger."

Chapter Sixteen

H is heart stopped beating for three full seconds before thudding back to life.

"How?"

"Lady Harriet attempted to hide the documents we brought in your room before she fled the estate."

"What do you mean, attempted?"

"She was interrupted by Stanhope's new valet before she reached your room. She had no choice but to hide and took refuge in Miss Catherine's chamber and secreted the documents there."

"Catherine's room?"

"Catherine?" Evangeline's eyebrow rose delicately at his familiar use of Miss Catherine's first name. Too late he realized his mistake. Inconsequential now in light of what Evangeline just told him.

"We have no time to parry. Did she say where she hid the documents?"

"Yes, in the lower drawer of Miss Catherine's desk."

"Did anyone see her enter or leave?"

"Not that I am aware. George…" Evangeline laid her hand on his arm when he made to leave. "The papers contain the names and identities of British soldiers who are on the Continent. If they fall into the wrong hands, they are as good as dead."

George shook off her hand and paced to the other side of the room, pushing agitated fingers through his hair. He faced Evangeline, her face pale and taut with worry. Her next words pierced his heart.

"Cavendish is on that list. You are the only one I trust implicitly. I know you will get these documents to the proper sources."

"He is alive?"

"It appears so."

"Thank God." His legs could no longer hold his weight and he collapsed into the closest chair. His greatest regret was leaving Devon Cavendish, the Earl of Anstruther, in France three years ago.

A few minutes later, after assuring Evangeline he would retrieve the documents, George slipped upstairs. Thankfully, no one spotted him in the servant's stairwell, nor the hall leading to Catherine's suite of rooms. He knocked softly and surprisingly received no answer. Maybe she hadn't escaped to her room as he'd deduced earlier. After he gathered the documents and placed them in safety, he'd begin a thorough search for her whereabouts.

Without making a sound, he slid into her room and immediately moved toward the desk. He first opened the drawer on the left, but it was empty and then the drawer on the right, also empty. Lady Harriet may have hidden the papers in the desk, but somebody had beaten him to it. He prayed it wasn't the Viscount.

CATHERINE

The light tapping of heels, echoing down the hall alerted George to someone's arrival. He closed the drawer and glanced around. As the bedroom door slowly opened, he stepped into the connected sitting room and pressed against the wall. There were times he cursed his large body, but he'd learned long ago that sometimes hiding in plain sight was the best recourse. With the door slightly ajar, no one would think anyone else was in the adjoining room. Once assured Catherine, or her maid could not see him, he'd leave through the door which led to the hall.

There was a rustling of skirts and the sound of pacing. He risked a peek through the crack of the door and saw Catherine, her mouth pursed into a tight line, walking from her desk to the fireplace and back again. Was she the one who found the documents, and if so, where had she placed them?

The door to her bedroom opened and he stiffened the same time she did. Whoever entered, their tread was heavy, purposeful.

"Do you always enter a lady's apartment without knocking?"

"Where are the documents?"

What was Stanhope doing in Catherine's room? Was she involved with his treacherous deeds? Had he misjudged her completely?

"I have no knowledge of what you are talking about?"

"Do not play games with me, my sweet Kitty cat," Stanhope snarled. "The whore was seen leaving your room. This is the only place she could have hidden them."

"As I do not know any woman of such ill repute, I am at a loss as to why you are here."

"You know *this* whore, you played with her when you were but a child."

"I have not seen Lady Harriet in over ten years, my Lord, and that was after you rendered her unconscious with a vicious blow to her head. However, if she is a guest and was seen entering my suite of rooms, she may have been lost. This is a rather large estate and it is so easy to lose track of where you are."

George was astounded Catherine had lied to protect Lady Harriet as she'd seen her not more than five months ago. He wondered again what the history was between them all and remembering how she'd blanched at the sight of Stanhope, knew it hadn't been pleasant.

"I always knew you were more cunning than you let on. Pity your father spirited you away so quickly the last time our paths crossed."

"My father has a capricious sense of timing. I thought he arrived at precisely the right time."

"Maybe we should renew our acquaintance now."

"Your taste runs to little girls with gap toothed smiles and falling ringlets. Surely I am too old for your certain proclivities."

Through the slim crack between the door and its frame, George watched as Stanhope ran his finger down the side of her cheek. Sickened by the familiar gesture, he wanted to turn his gaze away until he realized Catherine stared not at the wall, but at him, her eyes bright with unshed tears.

His pulse thundered through his body. She knew he was there, hiding in the next room, yet did not give him away to Stanhope. He flinched as though to move, to come into the room and stop this charade, but she shook her head slightly, her eyes silently pleading with him to remain hidden. When he acquiesced with a slight nod, she closed her eyes for one brief moment before sidestepping from Stanhope's reach, keeping her body between him and the door to the room where George stood rooted to the floor.

"There will be no further continuance of this, my Lord. I am no longer eight years old, unable to defend myself. Imagine the horror if this time I screamed and you were discovered in my chambers."

Bile rose in George's throat at the realization of what Kitty intimated hit him full force. Stanhope was even more depraved than he'd imagined. Preying on young girls at their most vulnerable. That Catherine was so sweet tempered and forgiving amazed him. His fist clenched and unclenched. All he wanted to do at this very moment was leap through the wall and choke Stanhope until he breathed no more.

"You think you can blackmail me?" Stanhope laughed, the sound bitter to George's ears. "I will tear your family to shreds. Even the great and mighty name of Darcy will not preserve you. All of England will know of your innocence lost. You are a nobody."

"What do you want?" she cried out. "I was but a young girl."

"Give me what I seek, and I will leave you alone. For now."

"Very well." Catherine turned until she again faced the room where George hid, her chin lifting with determination. Her life had just been laid bare by a despicable human being and still she protected him. "I placed the documents near Lord George's buttons. If they are not there, in a brown satchel, then someone has discovered and removed them."

She walked toward the window, drawing Stanhope's attention away from the adjoining room. George silently moved from behind the door and slipped into the hall. Thanks to Catherine's bravery, he had all the information needed to secure the documents. Later on, he would deal with Viscount Stanhope. He spotted a chamber maid near the top of the servant's stairs.

"You there," he called in a low tone so his voice wouldn't carry back to Catherine's room.

She turned and gave him a quick bob of a curtsy. "Yes, M'Lord?"

"Will you please knock on Miss Catherine's door and tell her that her father wishes to speak with her in the library?"

"Sir?"

He didn't wonder at her curiosity. Catherine's family wouldn't be arriving until tomorrow

"Just do this for me. Please."

"Yes, sir."

With haste he made his way down the servant's stairs and headed for the stables.

KITTY'S HEART SPLINTERED into a million pieces. She knew exactly when Lord George understood to what Stanhope had inferred by the dark shadow that crossed his countenance and the tightening of his lips. As much as she wanted to cry and rail at God for this painful secret being aired in front of a man she'd grown to love, she had no choice. When she'd discovered the satchel, she'd naturally opened it, finding reams of documents written in French.

At first the papers meant nothing, but then she's seen the name, Jonathan Lucas. He was on French soil as a spy for the crown and noted beside his name was his secret identity, Andre Brassard, a masonry apprentice. For reasons she couldn't fully understand, she trusted George more than anyone before and knew she had to get these documents to him as quick as possible. The house was not safe, so she'd chosen the one place only George, or a trusted servant would go - Button's stall. Near George's Buttons, she'd covered the satchel with straw.

She would suffer the ignominy of Stanhope's vile character to save the love of her life. Losing her reputation was a small price to pay for his safety.

"I trust you have all the information you require?" Kitty held her chin up with determination. This man stole her innocence at a tender age, but he would not make her cower in fright. The Lord was her strong tower and she mentally ran to the shelter her faith gave her. "I cannot help you further."

Viscount Stanhope assessed her, obviously deciding she'd told him truth.

"I will search Kerr's room. Pray they are where you said, or I shall return and make your life a living hell."

"The documents are exactly where I stated." She prayed hard Lord George understood her cryptic comment about Buttons. She counted on Stanhope not knowing the name of Lord George's handsome steed. Otherwise, all this subterfuge had been for nothing. Her attention was diverted by a discreet knock on the door. Stanhope moved to the wall so if the door opened he would not be seen.

"Yes?" Kitty called out.

The voice of the upstairs maid, Cassie, came through the wooden door.

"Your father wishes to see you in the library, Miss Catherine."

A wave of relief washed over her. Finally, she had a valid reason to leave and could escape Lord Stanhope's abhorrent presence.

"Thank you, Cassie. Please tell him I shall be there directly." She cut a glance at Stanhope. "Our discussion is finished, my Lord. Please leave my room."

"Pray to whatever god you hold dear that I do not have to 'visit' you again." The smile he bestowed on her was vile and her knees almost gave way before he turned and left the room.

She managed to stumble to her desk and collapsed into the chair, her breaths choppy and uneven. *Please God, help George find the satchel and save those men. Protect me from Lord Stanhope one more time.* She waited until her breathing evened out, then checked her appearance. Funny how serene her face seemed when her heart pounded with fear and anger.

She stood, shook out her skirts and proceeded downstairs toward the library. She knocked once on the door and hearing no one inside, opened the door slowly. The room seemed empty and she advanced a few steps. A footman came down the hall and Kitty stopped him.

"Have you seen my father, Joseph?"

"No, Miss. Your family hasn't arrived yet."

"Oh..."

"Can I get you anything, Miss Catherine?"

"What? No thank you. I must have been misinformed."

She dismissed him with a small wave of her hand and re-entered the library. Why would Cassie say her father wished to see her when he wasn't even here? Just then, a shot rang out.

GEORGE WHIRLED AT THE sound of a gunshot; the satchel slung over his shoulder as he made ready to exit Button's stall. Bless Catherine and her quick mind. Now he knew why she wasn't in her room; she'd been hiding the satchel.

He pressed against the wall of the stall and risked glancing into the stable. He had no way of knowing if the person out there with a gun was friend or foe. Relief at what met his eyes turned his knees weak.

The Honorable Colonel Richard Fitzwilliam stood over the prone body of Viscount Stanhope. Because of the lateness of the hour, the only staff member on hand was the head groomsmen, Dobson, with whom the Colonel was speaking with.

"What did you see, man?"

"He were goin' t'shoot Lord George."

Dobson still held the hunting rifle he'd used to kill the Viscount in his hand and George also noticed a dueling pistol on the floor near the still form of Stanhope.

"Send someone for Darcy and be discreet about it."

"I knew he were goin' t'shoot Lord George because he followed him in with the gun raised, and–"

"Dobson, I believe you and so will the magistrate."

"Yes, sir. Do ye need help with... with the body?"

"I shall help him," George said as he stepped forward. "And call for the magistrate."

"Yes, M'Lord." Dobson doffed his hat with respect and went to find Mr. Darcy.

When they were sure Dobson was out of hearing range, George requested the Colonel explain what he was doing.

"I was given a most interesting task this past summer. After an unnamed gentleman brought certain documents to Lord Grayson, he called me in to assist with what he called 'a delicate matter'. Imagine my surprise when I see documents linking Stanhope to France as well as a damning list, while no use in a trial by court as it held only initials and traces of conspiracy at the highest level, had apparently also previously been in the possession of Lord Jacobson."

"Fascinating." George murmured.

"Yes, it is. Further to this discovery, I also heard rumors of you scouting around Cambridgeshire in the guise of a chimney sweep. Not Lord George, thought I. What mischief was he up to? Imagine my surprise when I was made aware that the discovery of these documents coincided with your interesting foray into servitude."

Tired of being baited by the Colonel, who obviously knew everything he'd been involved with, George secured his hold on the satchel and wondered if he could gain access to his knife under the watchful eye of Darcy's cousin. Although the Colonel stated he'd been approached by Lord Grayson, he'd not told George he was on their side.

"What do you want, Colonel?"

"I want to congratulate you on a job well done."

George's mouth gaped open for a few seconds before he clamped it tight. He should have remembered how the Colonel liked to torment and tease. He'd been a master at the craft when they were but schoolboys.

For the first time in over an hour, the tension seeped out of his shoulders.

"Do not hand out your congratulations so quickly. We have no idea who his accomplices are." George muttered and looked down at the body of his greatest enemy on English soil.

"I have Stanhope's valet in custody and his other servants are being held in Lambton at the local inn. Grayson asked me to keep an eye on Stanhope. One of my men posed as his driver and I had reason to believe he had discovered you were the one who absconded with his booty. It was only a matter of time when he made his move."

"I thought I had time. I believed he would still be busy pillaging my room."

"He tried, but your door was locked. My guess is that he followed a hunch and came out here, and I followed him. Thank goodness Dobson was on the premises. All I have for a weapon is my ceremonial sword and it is back in my room. The worst I could have done was bean him over the head with a pail."

"I am forever grateful you had my back, literally."

"Think nothing of it. As you know, it is part of the job." The Colonel slapped him on the shoulder and also turned toward Stanhope's body. He cut a sideways glance at George and smiled. "Yes, I know all about your duty to King and Country. You have my undying gratitude for doing a job for which you are given no credit or accolades. Instead, people like me gain all the glory." He shrugged his broad shoulders. "Such are the vagaries of life."

"What of the book I passed on to Grayson?"

"That has become a bit of a conundrum. There are squirts and squiggles laced all through the book, but without a legend, no one can make heads or tails of it. Still, it gives the scholarly type of spy something to do on a cold winter's night."

"I cannot recall anything that would constitute a legend in the documents I left behind. There may be other hiding places. I only found the one."

"We hope to search his estate in the next few weeks. As it is, I now have to locate his daughter. Stanhope has been searching for her for about five years without success, and I am not sure we could do any better than the pack of wolves he hired to track her down."

George felt a true smile tilt the corners of his mouth, anticipating the Colonel's surprise at his piece of news.

"You need look no further than here."

"What do you mean?"

He gave a nod to a slight figure hurrying down the path toward the stables, a small bag in her hand. "Lady Harriet approaches as we speak."

"Son of a gun. I never saw that one coming."

Chapter Seventeen

"Papa went to Cambridge with Viscount Stanhope and they shared a love of antique books. The Viscount would visit Longbourn, not regularly, more like once or twice a year and Papa would grudgingly reciprocate. You know how much he hates to leave his book room."

It was past midnight and Lord George and Kitty were seated in the sitting room which adjoined her bed chamber. It was the one room where they were guaranteed privacy. He nodded at the apt description of her father. She knew most people thought Papa spent far too much time in his book room, but it hadn't always been like that. Prior to her fall from grace, Papa spent most evenings with the family, enjoying parlor games and listening to what each of his girls had done in the day. After... well, he retreated into his own world and Kitty now knew it was because he was deeply ashamed.

"The Viscount had a daughter, Lady Harriet. She was the same age as me, and when I got older, Papa would take me with him to Creighton Castle and we'd play together. The Viscount was always so attentive and I loved the singular attention."

"Why was that?"

How many times had she asked herself that very question? The answer had not come easy. She sighed deeply, stood and moved to gaze out the window, seeing nothing but bright moonlight caressing the cultured shrubs and trees. She didn't need to see disappointment mar his features.

"Jane and Lydia were Mama's favorite and Lizzy had such a unique connection with Papa. Mary kept to herself with reading and music. There was nothing which singled me out from my sisters, the exception being a persistent cough, which has thankfully stopped. I finally had something of my own. The Viscount never paid attention to my sisters the way he did me." She clasped her hands and squeezed them tight. "Oh, how I wish he had not."

"You were a child. You cannot blame yourself." Lord George came and stood beside her, the warmth emanating from his body both comforting and tortuous.

"No, but I blame myself for not running away. When he entered my room one night, I was so frightened. He held me down and I could hardly breathe. He was so heavy, I... I was only eight years old."

Lord George cursed Stanhope under his breath and she continued.

"He told me how powerful he was, much like he did tonight, and that he would ruin Papa if I ever told anyone. After...." she choked back a sob. Enough. Lord Jacobson had stolen enough from her. She squared her shoulders and lifted her chin. "After that encounter, we left the next day. At the time I was not sure if Papa knew what happened but have since found out he did. Regardless, we never visited the Viscount again and he never returned to Longbourn."

"Catherine, Stanhope will never harm you, or anyone else ever again."

"How do you know?" she cried out in real anguish, not registering that he'd called her by her given name. "He is a vile creature, too used to getting his own way. And he is rich, and powerful."

"Not powerful enough to survive a bullet."

Her startled gaze flew to his reflected one in the window. The gunshot she'd heard killed Stanhope? At her unspoken question, he nodded in the affirmative. Her shoulders slumped and with her face cradled in the palms of her hands, she wept softly.

Before she knew it, she was pressed against Lord George's broad chest, strong arms holding her close, his steady heartbeat a soothing balm for her tortured soul. She couldn't be sure, but she thought he pressed a light kiss to the top of her head before he released her and moved a few paces away.

"Get some sleep, my lo—" George turned his face away from hers. "Your family arrives in the early afternoon and the ball is tomorrow night. I know you want to look well rested and beautiful."

"How can I think of a ball when a man is dead?"

"Sadly, Miss Catherine, life marches on regardless of whether you dance or not. You may as well enjoy the moments you have and not regret what you cannot change."

With that, he gave her a polite bow and after checking to make sure no one was roaming the halls, exited her sitting room. As the door closed, she clasped her arms around her middle and squeezed, feeling more alone now than she'd ever felt in her short life.

Now he knew everything. Tomorrow, in the cold hard light of day, she'd find out if he still held her with warm regard or would give her the cut direct.

CHANDELIERS GLITTERED from the light of hundreds of candles and the musicians played softly in the background in preparation for the first dance. Nathan and Caroline would lead off the first set, along with Darcy and Elizabeth, Charles and Jane. If they so desired to dance, Mr. and Mrs. Bennet would join and George knew his brother Maxwell would have their mother on his arm. With no one in particular assigned to be his partner, he waited until Miss Catherine entered the room and moved toward her.

She looked positively regal in a light cream silk dress with crimson roses cascading down in a graceful swirl from her waist to the floor. Her bodice and sleeves had been trimmed in the same bold color. Matching flower buds were peppered through her mahogany curls, which had somehow been magically secured in an intricate manner atop her head.

The men of Hertfordshire, and more specifically the men of Meryton, were fools for not snatching this goddess up when they had the chance. He didn't care if people gossiped, but he planned on securing the first two sets with her, as well as the supper set. If he had his way, she'd sit out the rest of the dances in a dark corner. He had no desire to watch her on the arm of someone other than himself.

He knew when she'd spotted him approach. Her eyes widened, her mouth parted slightly – looking absolutely, positively kissable – and a becoming blush crept across her cheeks, giving them a rosy hue. All in all, she was absolutely captivating and one day, he'd make her his.

"Miss Catherine," he murmured as he took her gloved hand and bowed over it.

"Lord George," she returned with a polite curtsy, attempting to remove her fingers from his hold.

After a brief, silent tug of war, he let her go. The rosy hue had changed to two flags of color on each cheek. Adorable.

"If you are not otherwise engaged, may I solicit the first two dances?"

"Oh... I thought the first sets were for family only."

He could see that his request flustered her greatly.

"You forget, I *am* family. Nathan is my brother," he reminded her with a soft chuckle.

"But, is there not another lady of higher standing who should be your partner? Maybe Lady Cavendish, perhaps."

Ah... she'd had time to regroup from last night and now wanted to know what his relationship with Evangeline was about.

"Even though Lady Cavendish and I are *old* friends, she is not the one I wish to partner with. That honor belongs to you, and you alone."

She paused for so long George was afraid the music would start and they'd miss the first set completely.

"Yes, you may have the first two sets, Lord George."

Before she changed her mind, he plucked the dance card from around her wrist and scribbled his name beside the required dances. He also wrote his name next to the supper set. He longed to claim her for every dance, but even he knew that was ridiculous, although it was tempting – just to see her reaction.

The call for the supper set was announced, and George, who'd been standing next to Darcy moved to Catherine and offered her his arm. His mother, speaking with Lady Dalrymple, arched an elegant brow in his direction and he knew she'd have a few choice questions for him later on.

He and Catherine lined up with the other dancers and the strains of a waltz began playing. Holding out his hand for her, he drew her close and slid his other arm around her trim waist. The waltz wasn't as scandalous as it had been the year prior but having the chance to hold Catherine in his arms in an almost lover-like embrace was too good to pass up.

They began to move with the music and soon he realized she was counting softly under her breath. *1, 2, 3; 1, 2, 3;*

"Miss Catherine." She stopped counting and promptly stumbled. Quickly he tightened his grip and twirled her around to hide her small stumble. "Have you never danced the waltz before?"

"Is it that obvious? Miss Darcy and I practiced most of the afternoon and I was sure I had mastered the timing."

"You are doing magnificently. Have you noticed, since you stopped counting, that we have traversed the length of the ball room with no mistakes?"

"You must think me a silly goose."

"No," he whispered against her ear. "I think you are positively radiant and need to trust your intuitions."

With that, he twirled her around again and they danced in silence. At the end of the set, he offered her his arm and took her into the room set aside for supper, escorting her to the table where his mother sat with Maxwell.

"Miss Catherine Bennet, may I introduce my mother, Lady Margaret Kerr, Dowager Duchess of Adborough."

Catherine curtsied deeply and his mother gave her a polite, if somewhat regal nod. At his look of warning over Catherine's bowed head, she smiled. His mother was no fool, she knew this was the woman he'd chosen and would carefully interrogate her over supper. George planned on being right by her side and not let his loving family intimidate her in any way.

He excused himself to get them some punch and fought the mad panic that gripped his gut when he was delayed by slow moving guests. Frantic, he scanned the crowd for his table and almost stopped in his tracks at the sight of his mother laughing so hard, she dabbed at her eyes with a lace handkerchief.

Eyes bright with merriment, Catherine continued speaking, making small gestures with her hands. Every time she pointed to another part of her body Mother laughed a little harder. Even Max was having a hard time not to smile too broadly.

When he rejoined them, Mother held her hand out to him and he sank into the chair next to her, his and Catherine's punch still in his hands.

"Oh, dear George. Why have you not shared how you met Miss Catherine? I have never laughed so hard in all my life, except the time your father made me punish you boys for spitting paper wads at that horrid vase."

"We thought you loved that vase. You said it was priceless," Max said, his tone incredulous.

"That old thing? It was ugly and handmade by my crazy aunt who had fallen in love with all things from the Orient. My hope was you all would tear into the room one day and accidentally knock it over. Why else do you think I kept it near the door. With three boys, one of you were bound to kick the table in your haste."

"You made us polish all the silver in the house because of... *the incident*." Both George and Max said 'the incident' at the same time.

"That was also your father's idea. Even though we hated the vase, you all had to be taught a lesson in respect. Polishing the silver was my idea. You do not want to know what your father had in mind for your punishment."

"You are correct. I do not, although I imagined it would have involved our substantial stable and the removal of animal droppings." George mused out loud.

"I always knew you were a clever boy," his mother agreed. "I am of half a mind to put you to that task after the harrowing tale told by Miss Catherine. How you barely missed her head as you jumped over her at the last minute on your horse."

"Traitor," he said to Catherine, who'd listened to their conversation with rapt attention.

"I only repeat what my mother sees fit to share with all the principal families in our small village of Meryton."

"Oh no. This does not bode well for me." He absentmindedly held out her glass of punch.

"No, Lord George, it does not." Catherine smiled sweetly and plucked the glass from his hand. "Thank you for the punch."

How tall had the story become in the ensuing months since he'd attended Longbourn? Given Mrs. Bennet's bent for theatrics, he had a good idea everyone probably thought he and Buttons had trampled Catherine mercilessly and she nearly died. Fortunately, the Bennet's were headed home to Longbourn the next week and the neighbors would see for themselves that she was hale and hearty. Otherwise, there was no way he could safely show his face in Meryton without being run out of town.

"If I may lend some advice, Miss Catherine?" Mother leaned toward her. "I would hold out for a few more books for your father's library as recompense."

"I suggested to your son that he throw me into a pond when we were walking in the park a few months ago, assuring him that Papa would bargain for a new annex to house all the books coming his way."

"Oh, my goodness," Mother cried out. "I feel you have your father's wicked sense of humor."

"You know my father?" Catherine asked in surprise.

"Yes, as you were telling me your story, I remember my husband speaking of a Thomas Bennet he knew from Cambridge. Surely, they must be the same man. He always appreciated your father's quick wit and ability to recall any article or book he read. He said it was quite remarkable, that ability."

"I am pleased your husband knew my father. Over the years Papa's lost touch with many of his friends from Cambridge. Not for lack of trying on their part, but he preferred his books to society and everybody moved on with their own lives."

"How true, my dear. How true."

George marveled at where this conversation had led. Why hadn't Mr. Bennet told him he knew his late father? He'd have to ask him when he saw him next. Life had an interesting way of placing curves in the road and this was one of them. The other was the tacit understanding he and his mother had at this very moment. Given her delight in Catherine, he knew beyond a shadow of doubt, she approved his choice. Now all he had to do was convince the lady to become his bride.

Longbourn, early spring

For months following Nathan and Caroline's wedding, Lord George Kerr stopped at Longbourn on his way to Keswick Manor, and on his way back to London. He'd stay for a few hours each time and always ask if she and Mary would like to take a walk, or if the weather was inclement, spent the time having tea and gossiping with Mama and sometimes Papa.

He was all politeness and affability and Kitty wanted to kick him in the shins.

Then, he arrived on horseback right after dinner a week ago, a determined look on his face. Her mother almost bent over backwards in accommodating his every wish during his impromptu visit. What were his favorite foods? Did he like red wine or would he prefer port? Were his accommodations up to his standards? Did he prefer tea or coffee in the morning when he broke his fast?

And Papa. Who knew what he was up to. He actually stayed in the parlor with them each evening, eschewing his books and port and played cards! He and Lord George played chess, they played Backgammon, they rode around the estate, they even went fishing one day. They talked about his father, the former Duke, and Papa's university days.

Kitty was about to go mad from all of it as not once did he single her out for his attention. Even Mary admitted she had no idea what Lord George was up to.

Finally, she'd had enough. She grabbed Mary's book, *Sense and Sensibility*, and disappeared into the small garden at the back of the house. There was a nice quiet bench beneath the old oak, and she could hide there for a few hours in the world of Elinor and Marianne while the sun shone enough to keep her shoulders warm.

She'd read only the first chapter, developing a strong loathing for the Dashwood's half-brother when she heard the snap of a twig. Looking over her shoulder, her gaze lit upon Lord George leaning against the oak, strong arms folded across his chest, long legs stretched out before him, one foot casually crossed over the other. A deceptive picture of ease. How long had he been there, watching her?

Her breath hitched and by the glint in his eyes she knew he'd seen that. He was by far too observant, the wretched man. Here she was, trying to keep a sensible distance between them and he kept encroaching on her hard-won peace and quiet. Well, not so much peace, but it was quiet in this corner of Papa's estate.

Determined to ignore him, she picked up her book and resolutely stared at the page. Not one word filtered into her brain, but he didn't need to know that. The bench creaked from the weight of his body when he sat down beside her.

"With you I can have no secrets," he stated, out of the blue. "Up until this past year, I have been a spy for the King, travelling to France more times than I care to remember."

She gasped at his declaration and dropped the book onto her lap as she turned to face him. What other secrets had he kept from her?

"I aided in Evangeline's escape from France where we almost lost our lives and I lost my hearing for a few days when a musket went off right beside my ear. We set up a covert operation whereupon her husband, who stayed behind in France, forwarded us important papers. For over three years we dissembled information and saved the lives of countless men and women. I'm fluent in French, Spanish and Latin and can get by in German if they do not speak too fast." He stopped his narrative and she knew he was attempting to gauge her reaction. "That, dear Catherine, is my faithful narrative. You may confer with Lady Cavendish, although she will be more hesitant than I to share the details. Her husband remains on the Continent and she fears for his safety every day."

"Why are you telling me all this?"

"No secrets, Catherine. I want nothing between us that will cause regret or confusion down the road. No one has any power over us if they cannot threaten to expose what is known."

"But why?" she persisted.

"So that you will stop all this nonsense about not being a chaste maiden and marry me."

"I thought you only wished to court me."

"I have gone way past that and moved straight to marriage. I will take no risks when it comes to securing your affections."

Her heart soared, then plummeted like Icarus after flying too close to the sun. He may know her secret, but in reality, she wasn't worthy of being his wife. He needed someone he could be proud of.

"OH GEORGE, IT IS NOT only being unchaste. There are numerous reasons why I cannot marry you."

His chest tightened at her third refusal while at the same time his heart soared that she'd called him by his given name, not by his honorific.

"Yes, you can, and before you begin arguing," he said, holding up his hand to stop her protest, "let me say with unequivocal honesty, I know why we *should* not be married."

He suppressed a satisfied grin when her mouth, which had parted slightly to bring forth another argument, snapped shut. He loved when she did that. He rose to his feet and with hands clasped behind his back, more to keep himself from pulling her into an embrace than to present an imposing façade, he began laying out his reasons.

"I know our two social spheres are worlds apart and everyone expects me to marry someone from my tight circle of equals. I should scour the ballrooms of London and find a woman of my own class, someone who knows how my world works." He paused and took one of her hands in his. "But, why would I live in a world without you? My greatest desire is to be where you are. We shall create our very own world. The island of Kerr, and you shall be its queen."

"Even knowing my past, you truly wish to still marry me?"

"Yes. There is no one else with whom I want to spend the rest of my days. Besides, Mother told me I would be a fool to let you slip out of my grasp." Her small hand trembled within his and he dropped to one knee. "Catherine Eleanor Bennet, would you do me the extreme honor of becoming my wife?"

She stared down at their clasped hands, one lone tear streaking down her cheek and nodded yes. George gave her hand a tug so that she had to lean toward him.

"I did not hear what you said, sweetheart. Remember my one bad ear?"

"Yes," she finally whispered. "I will marry you."

He stood, bringing her up with him and crushed her against his chest, capturing her mouth with his before she became illogical and changed her mind. He almost patted his pocket to ensure the Special License remained safe, but decided he needed to kiss her one more time and it could wait.

"What would Mama say if she saw us now?" she managed to say between kisses.

"I am definitely not thinking of your mother at this very moment," he growled and tried to draw her close. She resolutely pushed at his chest and he looked down, pleased to see her cheeks so rosy. "Are you embarrassed, Miss Catherine?"

Eyes downcast, a small smile tipping up the corners of her lips, she replied, "Yes. You truly are a Rogue."

"I never was a rogue, my love." He kissed her forehead. "And if I had been, I would have given up everything for you."

"How can I deny you anything when you say charming things like that," she sighed out, lifting her face to his.

Not wanting to miss an opportunity to kiss her, he claimed her mouth. After a few delightful minutes he gently set her away from him. Eyes cloudy with desire, she blinked a few times.

"Before we get carried away, I must ask you a question. And seeing as you once stated you can deny me nothing when I am so utterly charming, I do not want to waste another second." He reached into his coat pocket and brought out the ring he'd purchased so many months ago. He took her hand in his, locked eyes with her and asked, "Will you marry me tomorrow?"

Her eyes shimmered with unshed tears and he thought she would deny him, again.

"Yes."

Prepared to hear a familiar 'No', he paused and opened his mouth to plead his well-rehearsed reasons of why they should marry tomorrow. Then, her soft answer filtered into his brain. She said...

"Yes?"

"Yes."

The ring was pushed onto her finger and her hand quickly enveloped in his. He tugged her down the path toward Longbourn.

"What are you doing?" Catherine asked, trailing behind, her arm extended.

"I am going to speak with your father before you change your mind."

"I will not change my mind," she said with a light laugh.

Abruptly he stopped and she bumped into his back.

"I cannot take that chance. I love you too much to let anything, or anyone come between us again."

With a quick pivot on his heel he started toward Longbourn, but this time slowed his pace and looped her arm through his. He didn't care who saw them because from now on this was her rightful place, next to his heart.

He looked down at his beautiful love, her cheeks rosy and a smile on her face. Lady George Kerr. He liked the sound of that. He liked it very much.

THE END

I hope you enjoyed reading George and Catherine's story as much as I did writing it.

I'm active on Facebook and Twitter.
Like or Follow to stay abreast of all things new and mundane,
about cats, about my grandkids, cooking shows,
reality TV, (don't judge), and my bi-annual vacation
For more information about my books, or to sign up for my
Reader's Club Newsletter,
visit my Facebook page

www.facebook.com/author/suebarr
www.suebarr.ca